LOSING SOLITUDE

Martin Murie
Feb. 23, 2001

LOSING
SOLITUDE

Martin Murie

HOMESTEAD PUBLISHING
Moose, Wyoming

ISBN 0-943972-34-5
Library of Congress Catalog Card Number 94-77619
Printed in U.S.A. on acid-free, recycled ❀ paper.

Published by
HOMESTEAD PUBLISHING
Box 193, Moose, Wyoming 83012

For Alison

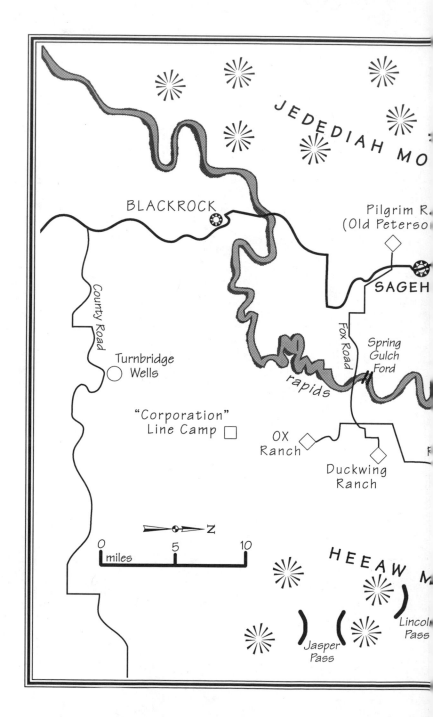

JEDEDIAH MO

BLACKROCK

Pilgrim R.
(Old Peterso

SAGEH

County Road

Fox Road

Turnbridge
Wells

Spring
Gulch
Ford

rapids

"Corporation"
Line Camp

OX
Ranch

Duckwing
Ranch

N

0   miles   5   10

HEEAW M

Jasper
Pass

Lincol
Pass

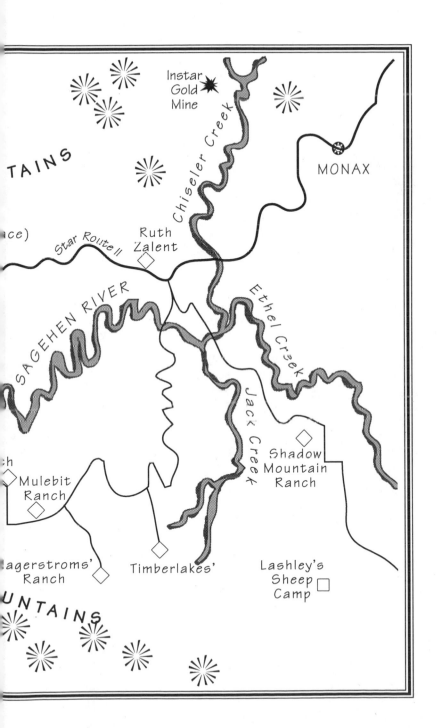

Losing Solitude

Chapter 1

....

TWO EAGLES DRIFTED TOWARD EARTH, and ravens rose as the eagles came in. The ravens flapped into an updraft, rode high, dropped suddenly to skim sage and saltbush, turning back toward whatever was dead on the ridge. Evan slowed, let the pickup come to a stop and waited for his dust to drift past before rolling down a window. The field glasses were at hand; he didn't use them. If a lamb or ewe was dead up there, he didn't want to know it.

Beyond the ridge were more ridges paling west to the Jedediahs. An intensity of haze marked the Instar Corporation's gold mine at the north tip of the range. Evan had been there, in the gullies and among the outcrops under tall, tawny cliffs streaked with grey. He had studied Jedediah forage plants and the pale subsoil, topsoil long gone. He had walked glumly across sectors so badly eroded they were nothing but auriferous gravel, and he had touched old stumps of juniper and pine, the saw cuts smoothed to velvety essences by a hundred-odd years of wind.

The pickup, dark green under dust. There is a shield on both doors, the words chipped by weather: U.S. Department of the Interior. Bureau of Land Management.

The driver, Evan Hughes, bureaucrat scientist. He's not yet comfortable in the role, maybe never will be. The sign on his office door at District Headquarters reads "Resource Manager," but out on the roads he's simply "the range con"—a federal presence.

Evan had been a young rancher, a man of parts: truck driver, animal tamer, mechanic, diplomat, reader of weather, pick-and-shovel man, bookkeeper and, in spare time, husband. He had been bushy-tailed, had given his all in the service of Hughes family holdings—1,600 acres and grazing allotments to match. Sixteen hundred acres of human intervention that had, in his view, gone haywire. He had walked away, from wife and parents, sisters and brothers, aunts, uncles, cousins and hangers on. Their eyes still glowed, even the dead ones, unappeased, hanging tough, proud on land they'd ravished. Evan's family. No worse than most, he believed. Better than some, for sure. There was no getting free of them; everything he admired and wanted could be found in those five generations of greedy thieves, if you looked long enough. And as time had passed, that spread of relatives back in Montana had grown in complexity; it was no longer flatly tragic. Sometimes, from inside the heat haze and the dust and rumble of his solitary journeys, Evan heard laughter. He remembered loving extravagance.

The rangelands had to come back, out of hard-nosed ownerships into something old and new, something Evan Hughes never dared to name. There had to be a turnaround, and he wanted to be in on at least the beginnings of that. This was a burning desire he held close. His office colleagues shared the same vision, in various ways and with reservations of one sort and another. He knew that; there had been conversations and remarks. But what else were they thinking and not saying? Even as Evan hid chancy thoughts from them, weren't they doing the same? Inevitably, he felt furtive. That was a bother, something to get used to. It went with the job.

Beyond the eagles' find, or kill, the road curved twice, then ran along an irrigation ditch that bordered a hayfield, bright oblong of order and hope. At the field's northwest corner, Evan turned off through a tall gateway of pine poles. The name board on the crossbar spelled, in faded black paint, "Shadow Mountain Ranch." The road crossed a quarter mile of willow tangle, an irrigation ditch and a short stretch of dusty greasewood before ending in a spacious yard backed by low dirt bluffs. Evan parked at the machine shed, a substantial building. One of the overhead doors was open, nobody inside. A pale yellow dog rose and walked stiffly into the hot sunshine. Stepping down from the cab, Evan took off his dark glasses, to avoid any hint of aggression. Knowledgeable resolve was what he hoped for.

Sudden sun glare made him dizzy; the scene turned dark. He bent and groped for the dog, found its muzzle, and the dog tongued his hand. The blackout began to ease, but oil-specked gravel still wavered and Evan looked into imagined long-ago dust and there were footprints—precise, morning fresh. Sheep and sheepdog. Herder and buckaroo. Coyote. Ute. Paiute. Shoshone. Evan stayed stubbornly still, kept his eyes blurred, brought up tracks of buffalo and wolf and the slither trace of a great sidewinder. He let them go, straightened, and faced the house. It was low and wide. There was a patio roofed with redwood slats, for shade, and flower beds fenced against dogs and livestock. A man stood in the wrap-around veranda. Manny Gabriel—tinted glasses, high-crowned black hat. He stayed there in the shade, watching.

Evan had forgotten his papers. He went back to the cab, reached in, and grabbed a manila folder. He crunched across the yard. "Another hot one, Manny. How's the boss?"

"He's all right." Manny's thin mustache barely moved.

Evan opened the screen door, stepped into the veranda, and waited with a smile, knowing Manny would make a show of slowness in opening the inner door. Manny had herded sheep for a good part of his life, most of it in Gino Donnadio's service. Now he was trusted servant/foreman whose duties at ranch headquarters were manifold and appropriately ambiguous. Evan knew that much about Manny Gabriel, nothing more.

Manny opened the door and murmured, "He knows you're here." The door had decorative bolt heads and strap hinges with beaten surfaces. Evan went in; his boots rang in the wide hall until he stepped onto the rosehip red and charcoal grey of a huge Navaho rug. Knowing the way, he turned left into Gino Donnadio's command post, a pine-paneled place of clean clutter. There were a few books in low shelves, a scatter of large black-and-white photos on one wall, each one framed. There was a portrait in oil of old Francis, a man who'd begun as a nobody, advanced to bronco specialist, and settled down in old age as a contract killer—coyotes, wolves, bobcats, mountain lions, eagles. Francis had ended his days on Donnadio's domain, an honored man, kind and cantankerous, with a reputation. Evan had missed knowing him by only a few years.

Gino Donnadio sat in a Naugahyde adjustable chair, one pale gouty foot propped on a stool, an aluminum tripod cane close at hand. A CB scanner stared with its red eye. Gino tucked his chin into his neck. "Well, sit down."

Evan took a cowhide armchair. He felt Manny's presence behind him, just inside the doorway. Evan put his folder on the coffee table. "Gino, you're looking good."

"I'll be around a while yet."

Evan's smile was stiff; he hadn't learned the light touch. Lately, he had been telling himself to go ahead and be a stick, the hell with it. "I've got to give you a deadline," he said. "Let's say a week from today. That'll be October the third."

Gino spoke past him. "Coffee, Manny?"

Evan heard Manny slip away. He opened his folder. "Transit rights from every outfit you'll cross along the way. Your copies." He dropped papers on the coffee table, they went limp across a *Cosmo* woman in gold lamé.

"Used to be, we'd do these things by word of mouth," Gino said. "We'd give our word. All these damned papers, this deadline shit, doesn't sit well with me."

"Fair enough," Evan thought, but he pushed on, reeling off names of cattle ranches on the east side of the Sagehen valley: TN, Two Diamond, Dew Claw, HT, Mule Bit, DuckWing.

Gino spoke. "I gave that Darwin a call. They're worse than BLM, down there."

"Couldn't be. Nobody's worse than BLM." This time, Evan's smile was real. "So, what'd Dave have to say?"

"Said he's confirming this thing. National Forest grazing. Said it was a concession to needs of BLM. Those are his words, not mine. Covering his ass at your expense." Gino's white eyebrows went up.

Evan nodded in agreement. He offered the transit rights; Gino hesitated half a moment before taking them. He let them cascade onto his side table. "I've filled in my lawyer on the situation. I don't know. There's some decisions I'll have to make. There's injustices here, no question about it. Like, you didn't give notice to Stallings, and everybody knows Stallings' range is as bad as anybody's. I won't say worse, I wouldn't say that about anybody's lease, but—well, enough said."

"Stallings' allotment is bad," Evan conceded, "but—and I've told this to every stockman in the district—all the leases are in terrible shape, and they've been that way since around 1890."

Gino held up a big pudgy hand. "Hughes, let me tell you, we sheepmen knew all this. We knew about the situation a long time back before these scientists got sent out and went to counting cactus and leaves of grass, counted every damned living thing and then some, picked up coyote shit, God knows what all."

Manny came in with coffee. He didn't offer cream or sugar. Gino was on a diet. Gino lifted his cup, studied Evan across the rim. Evan stared back, knowing he was being judged as a man who just might give ground. "Your Ethel Creek band has got to go into the Sagehen," he said. "That's the way it is. It's final. I'm sorry about putting a deadline on you; it's my way of saying we have a serious situation on our hands. I'm hoping you can take it in that spirit." His toes curled inside his boots, holding ground. "Ethel Creek has worst-case priority, I'm trying to be fair about this. Also, I'm forced to act on the basis of the riparian-areas preservation priorities."

"I've told you what to do with your riparian priorities."

Evan acknowledged with a stiff shrug. He sipped at Manny's black warmed-over brew. "That is not something I dreamed up, Gino. I have to administer it. I happen to agree with it."

Gino put his cup down. Coffee slopped across the transit agreements. "Let me tell you something, Hughes, about sheep. A band of sheep will spread out over their grazing; they know how to use it. But cows, they're a different case. A good part of the day, you'll find your cows piled up in the draws, wherever there's shade or a wet place. They'll chew bark right off the trees, they'll shit all over the place. A cow's a heavy animal. Just walking around, a cow will cut wet ground to pieces."

"Gino, for godsake, don't tell me about cows. I know about cows."

"Well, this is sheep country."

Evan put a hard grip on his coffee cup. "Down in the Sagehen, it's cattle. My district takes in a lot of territory. I've got wild horses to deal with, and goddamn burros. Antelope, mule deer, mountain sheep—what few haven't been poached off—and down around Goshen they're talking about llamas."

Gino showed no sympathy. "The Sagehen, that's a whole different thing."

"That may be, but the Sagehen's where those Ethel Creek woolies go. Now, as for your Shadow Mountain bands, I make no promises. We'll hope for the best. We'll see, next year. Remember, no promises." He took more paper from the folder. "Here's an overlay for the USGS map. I'll leave it with you. We're talking about 1,200 head of Ethel Creek sheep, right?"

"It was, before the coyotes and eagles got to work." Gino took a slurp of coffee, mouthed it, swallowed. "We had predators just about under control when these scientists started interfering. Kids, most of them. Dudes from back East. Women, too. Women scientists, picking up coyote shit."

Evan settled back and waited for the final litany he knew so well. It came. "All we need," Gino said, "is one year of normal rain. You'll see this country green up."

"Normal rainfall," Evan grumbled. "Lord almighty, Gino. You ought to know better. Normal rainfall in this part of the world is three, four years of dry and then, maybe, one of a little wet. That's what 'normal' is, and you know it."

They toyed with their cups. Evan tapped on the overlay with his ballpoint. "Scientific facts," he said.

"Except the facts you give me are cow facts, not sheep. I don't need all this Animal Unit Month stuff."

"I did not give you cow AUMs. I gave you sheep AUMs. Dammit!"

Gino changed the subject. "What do I do, a year from now?"

"Let's go over it. First, Ethel Creek might be showing some recovery by then, though I doubt it; but we can pray for a heavy snowpack and a wet spring. Second, by June next year, you have that band cut back to 850 head. Including lambs."

"You're trying to kill me. It's not legal, you know."

"Oh yes it is, and we both know it is."

A woman came in, quietly, and stood waiting, holding a big leather handbag. Her hair was puffed over her ears and waved back from her forehead like a shiny pelt with silver guard hairs. She wore tiny turquoise earrings. Evan stood and smiled and mumbled, "Mrs. Donnadio." Bea Donnadio always embarrassed him, there was something about her that reminded him strongly of his mother.

She returned his greeting and turned to Gino. "I might as well refill the prescription."

"I don't have it."

"You must have. You and Manny went to town last time."

"Ask at the drugstore, Jerry'll know about it."

They bickered amiably until Manny stepped to Gino's side table to fish out a slip of paper from a Louis L'Amour paperback. Bea laughed, glanced at Evan. "I'll have to take his bookmark."

"That's it," he thought. "Easy laughing over a nothing." Gino chuckled, soft and cool. Evan envied him.

Bea asked, "You want me to get you another book?"

"Sure, might as well."

"Louis L'Amour?"

"Doesn't matter."

"Oh my, such trust." Her soft, pudgy cheeks framed a quirky mouth. Evan felt sure that her trail hadn't been a single track, devotion to land and the man. She must have skylarked along the way, as she was doing now, making a light tripping adventure out of a hot boring twenty-three mile drive to town.

She went away, taking Manny with her, asking him something or other about the car. Evan stepped close to one of the photos on the wall, looked into faces of ten or twelve rough-trousered men. They stood in a line-up behind sheaves of dead coyotes. Round-brim hats, belt guns and rifles, plain-leather boots. Long ago scene, before the tight clasp of designer Levis.

"My granddaddy's crew," said Gino. "Just after the war."

"World War One."

"Oh my, yes."

"Big crews in those days."

"And hard work. Things are easier now." Evan had noticed it before, Gino's holding firmly to the present, apparently not bedeviled by nostalgia. Evan, though, still faced the photo, trying to penetrate its black-and-white moment. Was Gino's father one of those shy show-offs? Evan tried to imagine Gino himself as a lean youth, an up-and-at-'em stockman's son, tough as need be, and, eventually, winner of a skylark.

Gino said, "I'll try to meet your damned deadline. Under protest, that better be understood."

"It is. Don't worry, and in the long run you'll be glad." He went back to the cowhide chair, pleased with himself. But there was a dark side to it and Evan Hughes, MS, University of Wyoming, was man enough to admit to it, privately: Leonard Stallings' AUM ratings were bad, very bad. Politically, though, Stallings was strong. Evan was saving him for next year. He said, "When your herder moves into the Sagehen he'll be on the east side all the way. At the DuckWing's south gate he turns west, crosses at the Spring Gulch ford, drifts a couple of miles and he's home free. National Forest land, southeast flanks of the Jedediahs. He'll be surprised at the decent condition of that range."

"Yeah, I know. Old Peterson's allotment."

"It's held now by a stockbroker, somebody like that. New York City."

"I hear he's selling out."

"Yes, doesn't matter, he's relinquished his grazing lease. Dave Darwin handled all that. John Moss, you know him, manager on the Peterson place? Dave and I've been in contact with him, he knows you're coming." Evan stood. "If there is any problem, any problem at all, call Dave or me. We'll work it out."

"We'll see." Gino's hand drifted to the CB.

On his way out, Evan met Manny. They passed each other, each allowed a curt nod.

Chapter 2

 SAGEHEN, THE TOWN, is snugged up tight to the mountains like a thin buckle on a grey belt of sage. You can drive through on State Route 11 in about two minutes, from the View Motel on the north edge to the new Bureau of Land Management offices on the south. The BLM building stands well back from the highway, faced with pinkish sedimentary stone and isolated by a wide, well-kept lawn. There is a definite lonesomeness about it, an air of being different from anything nearby. About a quarter mile south of town a graveled turnoff dead-ends where a pair of Conoco storage tanks used to be. Couples park there, at night, and in the past two and a half years there has been a loner there, in daylight, between five and six thirty in the evenings, always in the same stance, his soft, fleshy body backed against the left front fender of his grey Toyota. Jerry Haun, Sagehen's pharmacist.

Facing west, he would let his gaze drift slowly across dark sentinel cliffs, from Wild Horse Canyon on his left, full of midnight blues and thick forest greens, to Gabbs Canyon on his right, wider and more gentle and swathed in sunset cross-lighting all the way to its first turning amid scrabbles of talus, fir, whitebark pine, mountain maple shrubs that blazed red in the fall. Peace came quickly or not at all. When it did, Jerry Haun's lowly life drew back for a while, had to let him go. He hadn't studied to reach such blessedness, it had come unsought, a gift. He wasn't aware of any particular discipline on his part, he simply leaned on the fender and it happened, or it didn't. When dry night rose up from hayfields and sage flats of the valley behind him it gave him a gentle shock, as a force from outside. That's what the blessedness was all about.

The Toyota was always with him. He could have walked to the Conoco turnoff by way of the westside trail, seldom used. It would have been a private and pleasant walk and he could have used the exercise. But Jerry had never set foot on that trail, he knew it was there, but vaguely.

It was understood, Jerry Haun had a thing about the Jedediahs. People accepted that, it was OK to have, even to show, respect for the Jeds, and for the valley, for all of the Sagehen. And they all needed Jerry Haun. Everybody came to him, in time. Vincent Van Horn, his employer, had understood how it would be. Need was the name of the game. "Oh, he's a little strange, in some ways," Van Horn admitted, "but Jerry is a man who knows his trade, make no mistake about it. And you can trust him." Then, with a chuckle, "You'll damn well have to."

They did come to trust him, they learned that secrets encoded in doctor scrawl were safe with him. While learning that, they kept busy sizing him up as to other things that mattered. It was confirmed that he did truly live alone, night and day. He kept one cat, he shunned intimacies, hardly ever traveled. The community, in its normal underhand fashion, created a role for their pharmacist: Sagehen's eunuch. A narrow niche, but safe enough, and it conferred a near invisibility. People often held private confabs within earshot of Jerry, as if he wasn't there. He absorbed such disdain, kept their secrets.

It was midmorning at Vincent Van Horn's Rexall Drugs. Ruth Zalent and Belle Izard stood near Jerry's counter, Ruth carrying on, actually ranting, about a new development called Far Haven. Jerry knew little about Ruth Zalent. She was a relative newcomer, from back East, a pleasant, harried-appearing woman. Twice, she had brought him an order for antibiotic prescribed by the dentist in Goshen. As for Belle, Jerry had more on her than he wanted.

Belle interrupted Ruth. "Not the whole valley, you always exaggerate."

Ruth shook her head, vehemently. "Not true, not true." She began to list Far Haven's goals. "World class ski center, trails and lifts and all that; some kind of Alpine Village affair, you can just imagine. Airport, of course, over on the east side. And a gondola to the very top of the Jedediahs. They have the name picked out."

"Name for what?"

"The goddamn gondola."

"Ruth, where do you get all this information?"

"Oh, all over. I read a lot, I listen to the radio."

"You'd think our *Courier* would have it first, wouldn't you?"

"Yes, you would. Want to know the name of the gondola? It's 'Rise to the Western Sun.'"

"That's a little fancy, don't you think?" Belle was smiling.

"Fancy? Oh, Belle! Obscene is the word. They're serious men, though. They will do what they say they will." She went on with her list. "Golf course and a grand hotel, a dam on the river to make a landscaped lake. Condos on both sides of the river. Boats, naturally. Canoes, riding stables."

"It's all hard to believe."

"Lots of things are hard to believe, Belle, but they do come to pass. Strip mines, uranium mines, nuclear power plants. These do come to pass."

Belle shook her head. "I hate to see you so upset. It's not all bad. Do you know the part that bothers me the most? That hotel, right smack dab in front of Wild Horse Canyon. Red and I've gone in there, in deer season. It's a lovely place."

"Oh, I know it. If I had the money, know what I'd do? Buy one of those open space easements for Wild Horse."

"Ruth, I do have to say it, a lot of folks are really excited over this Far Haven business. I mean, they're favorable to it."

"Please, Belle, I understand. Cash flow is important, it's vital. I was a Certified Public Accountant in my other life, did you know that?"

"Well then, you know a lot more about all this than I do, but Ruth, maybe you haven't been here long enough to realize Sagehen is practically a ghost town. We need *something*."

Ruth, trying her darndest to be a good sport, gave Belle a wide smile. "It's one of those paradoxes," she said. "Sagehen being practically a ghost town was precisely the reason I settled out here, bringing my meager spending power."

"Ruth, I have to run. Take care. Anyway, it's beautiful weather."

"Gorgeous, and here it is, almost October."

Belle left and Ruth stood still, trying to remember why she had come into Van Horn's. She had made a shopping list, but left it at home.

"Mrs. Zalent?"

She looked up. Jerry Haun, moving little plastic containers from one place to another on his glass-topped counter, asking, "How much would it cost?" Ruth noticed that the thin black frames of his glasses were a perfect match for his eyebrows and lank hair that went sparsely back over a pale scalp, dramatizing the pudgy white face. She said, "Are we talking about the same thing?"

"Wild Horse Canyon."

"I don't know, Jerry. More money than any of us could lay hands on. It's not for the likes of you and me."

"Too bad."

"We could always rob a bank."

His mouth stretched into a thin line ending in fat cheeks, his shoulders made an awkward dipping motion. He repeated himself. "It's too bad." A customer came to the counter and Ruth moved away. She walked slowly down one of the aisles, reading labels mindlessly. There it was: hot water bottle. She took it to Flora Kimball at the front checkout.

At 11:50, Jerry wandered past Flora Kimball's station. The store was empty of customers. He stopped at the front window and looked past the magazine rack. "What do you make of this Far Haven thing?"

She laughed. "I'm not paid to think."

"The Sagehen's all set to boom and blossom, Flora. Your wages might go up."

"Hey, Jerry, there's something you forget, I am about to marry the boss man. How come you keep forgetting?"

"Why does she keep on about that?" he thought, even as Flora silently condemned herself for that very thing. "Hasn't Jerry told me how happy he is for me? Didn't he tell me Vince was a good man? Yes, he did—in a mumbly way, but that's Jerry, that's his way. And when I hinted around about the big age gap, Jerry didn't hem and haw, he came right out, said, 'Flora, you go right ahead, it will be fine.'" Still, she waited, wanting him to say all those things, all over again.

Jerry and Flora, they'd spent many a dull slack time in the big, cluttered store, going into and out of halting conversations. Flora was still vaguely disturbed by him. His reticence, so extreme, she assumed it must be a cover for something pretty weird. Sometimes she was simply mad at him because he refused to take any interest in trading secrets. She didn't want many, and they could be little ones and from way back, hers from Twin Falls, his from Pocatello. They'd grown up in the same state, the south half at that, and didn't that make them fellow clansmen, Snake River people? Apparently not. At least he was evenhanded about it, treated his boyhood as no more interesting than her girlhood.

Without some trading, though, how could you get on with anybody? And yet, there was this paradox: Flora had come to depend on his not delving. That strangeness had gradually put more free and easy space between the two of them, and she knew it. And, he had never raked her with his eyes. Not once, so far as she knew. He had never tried *anything* with her.

She tossed back her long, blonde hair and reached for a cigarette. "Jerry, something's on your mind."

"Not a thing."

"Liar."

He looked away, his smile thin, sheepish. "You heard about that hotel they'll put up at Wild Horse Canyon?"

"Yes. More than a hotel, practically a little town is what I hear, but everything's to be natural. You know, spread out, sort of low, to blend in with the environment."

His thick fingers tapped lightly on the magazine display and he made no comment.

"Jerry, I don't understand mountains," she said. "I mean, I don't get with them the way people like you do, but I like them, I think they're great."

"Everybody does, I guess."

That was insulting. "Hey!" she said, and waited until he turned to her and she said, "I've been back in there. Gabbs Canyon. Winona Turpin and me, we had a wonderful time."

They were looking hard at each other and, for once, he didn't waver. She smiled. "So, don't treat me like some dumb dude."

"OK," he said. "You know something? I've never been in the Jedediahs."

"Really?" She thought, "Now we're clickin'." But a car door slammed, in the parking space behind the store. They waited, the back door opened and Vincent Van Horn was there, a virile, florid male, upright, solid of belly and shoulders and thighs. Hair white, cared for, eyes grey. Vincent Van Horn was, people said, the handsomest over-fifties gent in all the Sagehen. He carried a briefcase under one arm. He unlocked the office door and disappeared. Jerry returned to the pharmacy. In a little while Van Horn came out of the office and went to Flora. "Hold the fort," he said, "I'm headed back to Goshen. Hell's a poppin'."

"Far Haven stuff?"

"You got it." He winked and put a hand on her shoulder. They looked at each other, she asked, "Problems?"

"The kind I like. We're on top of it."

At twelve o'clock Flora went home for lunch. Jerry stayed near the front of the store. Wednesday, a slow day. He wandered the aisles, picked up a hairbrush somebody had knocked off its peg, realigned shampoos and oils and sprays. When he came to the magazine rack he stared for a while at the front page of the *Sagehen Valley Courier,* last week's, the headline four days old: "Far Haven Surveyors Roam Valley." The front windows darkened, in another few moments rain slicked the glass, worked into a whispery beat on the pressed metal siding of the ancient building. Van Horn's had once been a general store. Before that, who knows?

Across the street two young couples in bright Lycra outfits stood under the peppermint awning of Mountain Bike Shop. Their bikes were slotted into the shop's rack. One of the couples made a sudden dash across the street and into the drugstore. The woman asked, "Isn't this the place where you get the ice cream sodas?"

"In Goshen," Jerry said. "Twenty-seven miles."

"It's called Nineteen Twelve? And they do have the old-fashioned kind?"

He nodded. "You turn left at the first light. There's only three lights in town, you can't miss it." He gave these directions often, the fame of Nineteen Twelve, an oasis in the desert, having spread far beyond that of its town. In fact, Goshen had no fame at all, it was merely a county seat nobody had ever heard of. But Nineteen Twelve had an authentic marble-top fountain, a floor of black and white tiles, tables and chairs of twisted metal. It had a full range of sodas and shakes and sundaes, all served in glass, nothing styrofoam in there. And all transactions were rung up on a noisy bronzed NCR machine. Jerry said, "You might try the Green River Float."

"Hey, I've heard of it."

Her companion had gone to the door, he had his hand on the bar. "Come on, Sue."

"Tom, please. Don't keep doing it, OK?"

"The rain's quit," he said.

She turned back to Jerry. "This town, why's it called Sagehen?"

"I don't know. Sage hens are a sort of grouse."

"Oh yes, like partridge. Is it a real cow town?"

Tom moaned, mouthed a few words.

Jerry hesitated, said, "It is a cow town. I don't know how real."

Her eyes widened, her smile was quick. "Did I ask a stupid question?"

"No, no, not at all." He looked to the back of the store, to the pharmacy, as if for help.

She persisted. "Something to think about, right?"

Chapter 3

 VAN HORN RETURNED at a little after four. He called Jerry into the office and closed the door and locked it. The room smelled of cigar smoke and men's lotion. Van Horn plunked himself into his chair and took a briefcase from the top right-hand drawer. Jerry sat down in one of the two straight-back chairs in front of the desk. Van Horn unlocked the briefcase and dumped out a plastic bag. He unsealed it and, with a flourish, poured bundles of green-backs across the desktop. One bundle bounced to the floor, Jerry picked it up. "Good Lord," he said.

Van Horn gave him a grin. "Nice, eh? Well, back they go. Give me a hand."

Jerry held open the plastic bag, Van Horn packed it, laying the bundles with care, squaring them. "This kind of work I don't mind." He rummaged in the bottom drawer of the desk, came up with a brown paper grocery sack. He put the plastic bag into that and made it up into a tight bundle and secured it with parcel post tape.

Jerry stopped watching. His gaze was moving along the baseboard, slowly, as if he had seen a beetle or a timber ant down there. It was a habit that puzzled and irritated Van Horn, but at the same time he took it as verification: such abject diffidence surely must be an expression of dog-like obedience. He said, "It goes to JT Timberlake. Can you handle it?"

"Uh, sure Vince. I assume this is an anonymous contribution of some sort."

"It is. Something wrong with that?" He opened his cigar box. "Actually, anonymous is not exactly the right word."

Jerry managed a quick face-to-face glance at his employer, readying himself to say, again, that he would handle it, no problem. Van Horn, misinterpreting, went on the defensive. "Jerry, you don't think I'd ask you to do something not quite square with the law, do you?" He clipped a cigar and lit up and tried to puff away his annoyance. "Damn it all," he was thinking, "can't this pharmacist put on a bit of man-to-man savvy?" He tried again. "Jerry, the picture is this: I want JT to know who's relaying this packet. That's important to me, and to Smoke Creek, just now."

"I see. You don't want to be too obvious, though."

"Exactly. JT knows you, Jerry. Everybody does. He'll know who you're with, where you come from. There'll be no need for any big conversation. Pleasant greetings—blah, blah—no sweat. He'll understand. You free tonight?"

Jerry nodded. Van Horn took the money to the safe. "It will be here when you lock up. The combination's the same as always."

"The money's not yours, Vince? Personally, I mean? Smoke Creek business, right?" He was referring to Smoke Creek Land and Cattle Company. Van Horn was their Ponera County agent: he covered a large territory, from south of Goshen north through all of the Sagehen country to Monax and beyond. He had had a marvelous flurry of transactions in the past few months, most of them in connection with Smoke Creek's contract with Far Haven.

Van Horn said, "Smoke Creek, of course. What we have here is a collection of normal, voluntary contributions from various individuals and firms. Nothing new, Jerry. Routine. I wanted it to be Smoke Creek's turn to make the arrangements."

Jerry understood. James Terril Timberlake published a monthly newsletter, *Free Range*, and he would be running for Congress next year and it was only natural for firms and individuals of like mind to gather around to help him to a good running start. They were serious and so was JT, he meant to win. His supporters understood that, and the need for more than token aid.

Jerry, at the door, hesitated again. "So, I'll just say I was passing by and thought I'd drop this off."

"Exactly."

Jerry found himself staring at the dull beige door frame. Why had this happened, today of all days? "Does JT know how much money's in there?"

Van Horn chuckled. "He will when he counts it. Now look, this is not one of those errands people write down in ledgers and log into computers and tell their secretaries to make a note of. Misunderstandings can pop up, so damned easily. Unbelievable, you'd be amazed."

"Sure, Vince. So I don't ask for a receipt."

"Honest understandings is what this is all about. Listen, if you'd rather not, tip me the nod. I can make other arrangements." Van Horn's face had reddened.

"No, don't worry, Vince. I'll take care of it, tonight."

The Timberlake place nestled between two low ridges in the northeast reaches of the Sagehen Valley. It was a garden spot in a dry, crusty land. There were cottonwoods and willows and a strip of lawn and the sound of a tiny creek that had been made by diverting an irrigation ditch.

The ranch was only six years old. Althea and JT had built it from scratch, using profits from his law practice. They didn't run cattle, but Althea raised horses. They both rode out on pack trips, twice a year, sometimes oftener. They carried guns, always, for "predators," meaning coyotes, porcupines, woodchucks, badgers, ravens—and once they'd taken a bobcat. And if an out-of-season mule deer happened to show up within range and at a convenient location, well, what the hell. Althea and JT were right-intentioned people, they'd earned every cent of what they had, they loved the land and knew how to use it properly.

Jerry didn't get there until well past eight o'clock. A half moon lighted the pair of ornamental blue spruces at the front entrance. There were swatches of moon silver on a dozen or more cars parked at various angles; some of them had their noses on the lawn, the driveway was so crowded. The east windows were alight. Jerry parked and stepped out. Had Vince known JT and Althea would be throwing a party? Probably not. Maybe it would be best to come back tomorrow. No, get it over with. A dog trotted from the front porch, Jerry waited, the dog checked him out. Jerry crossed the lawn and peeked into a room alive with festivity, animated clusters of people, the men in informal dress, the women moderately dolled up. Heads of animals dominated one end of the room, above and on each side of a fieldstone fireplace. In front of the fire screen, a grizzly bear rug, and high up, soaring just below exposed rafters, a golden eagle. Jerry remembered that eagle; JT had shot it, from the deck of a helicopter. He had been arrested, paid a big fine. Then, somehow, the eagle's carcass had been retrieved from the state's Fish and Game freeze locker. The caper had earned JT a mixed bag of publicity, most of it favorable. Subscribers to *Free Range*, imagining themselves beleaguered—environmentalists on one side of them, feds on the other—took the eagle incident as one more proof that JT was the man they needed.

Jerry returned to the car, followed by the dog. He opened the trunk and stood there for a long while contemplating three paper bag bundles. Finally, he chose one of them, closed the trunk lid on the others. He half-circled the house, following an odor trail of roast beef and browned potatoes. The kitchen door was open. Inside, a big, bald-headed man stood in front of a wood-burning range. He noticed Jerry, called out, "You missed the feed. I could rustle you up something."

"No, thank you," Jerry said. "I was driving by and thought I might see Mr. Timberlake, for just a minute."

The cook gave him a quick once-over. His face was weather-beaten, permanently so. He said, "I fixed them up a meal. Now it's my turn. Come on in."

"I'm Jerry Haun, I work at Van Horn's."

"Sure, I recognize you now. I bought some medicine off of you. Kundermul."

"*Kondremul*, yes."

"Great stuff, did the trick. I recommend it to all my friends. Here, I'll get you a drink."

"No. I—well, OK."

The cook reached deep into a cupboard, found a bottle of Wild Turkey. He poured a shot for Jerry and replenished his own. "Here's to crime."

Jerry blinked, eyed his glass, turned to the sink to add water. The cook noticed the package held tightly under Jerry's left arm. "Medicine, eh?"

"Yes. Do you suppose you could get hold of Mr. Timberlake? I need to deliver this to him, personally."

"Personally, eh? Well, piss my pants." He adjusted the damper on the stove. "This is the best kitchen I ever had. Got everything I want, and the flies and mosquitoes and cranky cowpokes stay outside. I've seen the worst, believe me. Well, that's all behind us." He lifted his glass and glared. "Any complaints?"

Jerry sipped at his drink, said, "This is good," and meant it. He drank more, studied the wood box and the far corner where three mouse traps were placed in a pattern that covered all approaches.

The cook said, "I see you're the type that doesn't go in at the front door unless they're asked. No offense, but I see that's your style."

"I guess it is." Jerry drained his glass.

"All right, I can take a hint. You're in a hurry." He hid his glass in the cupboard, selected a teacup, mixed himself a slurry of water and baking soda. He rinsed his mouth, threw the rest of the freshener down the sink. He took off his apron, wiped his mouth with it, straightened his collar. "I'll go get him for you."

Jerry rinsed his glass under the hot water tap and put it in the dish drainer. He waited. There was still time to back off, but the whiskey glowing across his middle made a small difference, perhaps the crucial difference, who can say? Timberlake came in, a heavy man in his late forties, radiating hearty well-being. Automatically, his hand was out and Jerry took it, then gave him the package.

JT said, "Jerry Haun, you're with Van Horn."

"Yes."

JT fished a slender clasp knife from his pocket. He slit some of the tape and brown paper, took a look inside. He glanced at his cook, who had his back to JT and was running dishwater noisily.

JT said, "Just what the doctor ordered. Thanks, Jerry." Again, he offered his hand.

North of the Timberlakes', the county road is a bad one, dangerous in wet weather. Its gravel washboard loops into steep gullies, takes sharp turns around tips of ridges, its shoulders are barely there. By the time Jerry reached the asphalt of Highway 11 he had racked up nearly an hour of concentrated driving that had kept his anxiety at bay. But now, the Toyota humming smoothly south, he began to shake his head. He looked for a place to turn around, to get back to the Timberlakes before they went to bed. Suddenly, there it was, Ruth Zalent's mailbox, the name in scrolled letters, like a command in the headlights' glare. Jerry cut the motor and glided into Ruth's driveway. When he opened the car door the smell of rabbit brush made him sneeze. He unlocked the trunk. Sickened by indecision, he no longer hesitated. In less than half a minute the two paper bag packages had been stuffed into the mailbox and the Toyota was on its way.

Around the next bend, Jerry braked to a quick stop. He scrambled into tall weeds and sage and rabbit brush, took a few steps, came up against a barbed wire fence. He unzipped and let fly.

Back at the car he turned, crossed his arms, faced the Jedediahs. They looked strange and not only because he usually looked at them from a more southerly position. No, something had gone wrong and the reason was all too obvious: the stealing of ninety-thousand dollars from JT Timberlake. The intent had been pure, nothing more nor less than the rescue of his mountains, but now, there, in bright moonlight and splendid in silent power, those mountains stood stubbornly aloof. They had lines across their flanks that Jerry had never seen before: map lines. "Good Lord," he said. He had dropped an ante at the high stakes table, taken a seat in the game of boundaries and jurisdictions, and ruined everything.

Chapter 4

....

 THE HEADWATERS OF Ethel Creek are eighteen miles north of Sagehen Valley, in high desert where mesa rimrock sheds talus the color of milk chocolate, making scree patterns that are visible from miles away: letters and animals and mysterious symbols, they last for a long time because the rock breaks down so slowly into soil, but replenishment from fresh rockfall does change them. One such figure is a proud high-stepping camel with two humps and five legs. Go south, the camel turns into a fat hen. Go north, it doesn't look like much of anything. You might wonder about the camel's age. Maybe, one time, a band of bow hunters or a war party or a group of women scraping hides at the head of Ethel Creek looked up and smiled and named it, but that wouldn't mean any more to us than "Ethel Creek" would to them. No, the camel probably wasn't even there, that far back. Was it a cave bear, then? Giant sloth? Bulldozer? By the way, who was Ethel? Wife of a surveyor? A name in a book? Nobody seems to know. Strange sound, "Ethel Creek."

When you climb about halfway to the camel and look down you see a half acre of emerald green water-loving plant life spread out in a seep that freezes in winter and brims over in the spring. Every summer the mud goes half dry and cracks, making cakes with dusty tops, perfect registers for delicate signatures: kangaroo rats, deer mice, sage hens, pack rats, mourning doves, sage sparrows and others. Sheep, antelope and coyotes make deeper prints; these collect windrift, tiny desiccated bits of desert, such as beetle legs, saltbush spines, wild rose petals. There is a grove of cottonwood and low willow where migrating warblers stop for a day or two. On the brush slopes above, green-tailed towhees.

The water collects in little channels that join and meander west toward Monax, a sheep town for most of its life, more recently a gold mine base. You won't see Monax, it's behind a distant mesa that has no name. The creek turns in wide sweeps, trending south. It looks like a willow-green hyphenated thread on a vast sage sea. Far off on the sea floats a mesa, Gore Mountain, much like an aircraft carrier looming on the horizon. Alongside Gore Mountain the creek gathers strength from a number of sheep-trodden seeps, and below Gore's west prong the water becomes lively, sparkles across gravel bottoms. There are trout in deep eddies. A headgate shunts some of the flow into an irrigation ditch near the headquarters of Bea and Gino Donnadio's Shadow Mountain Ranch. Beyond Donnadios', three more sheep outfits take water, most of the deficit being made up by Chiseler Creek, from the Jedediahs. Chiseler Creek is suspect, accused of bearing a taint of cyanide from Instar Corporation's heap-leach process gold mine. The Donnadios are sure there's nothing wrong with that water. "It's still good old mountain dew," they say. "Environmentalists spread these rumors, there's no real evidence." They have a point: nobody has offered gold enough to buy year-round monitoring of cyanide parts-per-million in any section of the Jedediah watershed.

Farther south, Ethel Creek picks up Jack Creek; together they make a stream too wide to jump across, the Sagehen River. State Route 11 approaches the river at that point and enters a wide valley, cattle country: the Sagehen.

In this northern part of the valley one of the few lived-in places, aside from ranch headquarters, belongs to Ruth Zalent, a newcomer. If you happen to drive Route 11 you won't know Ruth is there, except for the mailbox and scarcely noticeable driveway. Her three-room prefab hides in a grove of aspen and serviceberry a hundred yards from the highway. During Ruth's first summer in the Sagehen, a friend from New Jersey stopped by for a visit. She left a day early, with a warning. "You can't go on living here."

Ruth replied, "You're probably right."

She stood now at her CD player, making adjustments. The volume setting was higher than what had been normal back in New Jersey. Ruth couldn't live without music, but nowadays music had an additional function for her, it was a shield against the gold mine. Her purchase of six hideaway acres in front of this fantastic mountain range had turned out to be one of the worst moves in a career crammed with error. The Monax realtor had known, but hadn't breathed a word about Instar Corporation. He'd spoken of environmental serenity, lying in his teeth. He'd said, "serenity" at least half a dozen times. Ruth should have been more than amused.

She'd barely tasted the beginning of new freedom before the mine set forth on its fifteen- to twenty-year assignment, the nibbling into rubble of two high Jedediah ridges. Ore trucks, ore stampers, diesel-powered generators, drill rigs, dozers and loaders disturbed the air and the ground, seven days a week, except in the worst of winter. The intrusion was subtle and varied. "Plain honest racket would be one thing," Ruth raged, "but this beast is sly. Sometimes he nearly sleeps, sometimes he rears up and roars. I never know what to expect."

Martin
Murie

38

Her nearest neighbors, a sheep herder and his family over on Jack Creek, agreed that the mine could be a nuisance, but they assured her that they didn't really hear it very often, they'd adapted. Ruth couldn't believe that; she was sure they were lying to themselves, keeping up some sort of macho pretense; or else they had handed her a sneaky comment on East Coast sensitivities, environmental la de da.

She stretched out on the couch, reviewing the past twenty-four hours. The fuel oil hadn't yet been delivered. She'd spoken too vehemently to her friend, Belle Izard. There were mule deer prints in the driveway dust. And another kind of track, also in dust; a clawed animal, fairly large. Badger ? The violins came in alone and Ruth drifted. The phone rang. She tumbled from the couch, cursing.

"Yes?"

"There's something in your mailbox."

"What ? Who's speaking, please?"

"Go to your mailbox."

"Who is this?"

"It's important, for Wild Horse." The line went back to humming.

Ruth ruffled her short black hair, cursed some more. She went outside and picked her way down the long bumpy driveway. Her building contractor had argued forcibly against a hundred yard setback from the highway. "Convenient access is awfully important, especially in winter." He'd been right, and the power and phone line extensions had been terribly expensive.

The mailbox held two packets made of paper bags sealed with tape. Ruth pulled away some tape, opened a bag, turned it until it filled with moonlight and gasped. Recovering, she said, "Oh, a joke." She started for the house, wondering if she was now obliged to figure out a response to the joke, but then she remembered the phone caller's last words: "For Wild Horse." She looked again into the paper bag, reached in and pulled out one of the packs of bills. Franklins, every one, looking awesomely authentic. She ran into the house and locked the door. She knelt at the couch and began to count. She could feel the mine's throbbings under the floor, deep in the earth.

"We're all crazy," she whispered, "every one of us." She rocked back on her heels, stared into a dark corner. Finally, she rose and went into the kitchen to look out, toward the mountains. She was feeling resentful of this new intrusion into her life, but as she scanned the rough ridgelines and foldings of the Jedediahs' lower slopes she felt a rush of gladness. She tried to visualize Wild Horse Canyon, the deepest and, people said, the wildest in the range. For a few moments Ruth Zalent felt twenty years younger.

"All right," she said, "one last stand, before Instar puts me under."

Chapter 5

WILLOWS AND NATURAL hay meadows fit the lazy winding of the Sagehen River. The meadows have straight sides where they meet alfalfa fields. Further east, these lush spreads of alfalfa end abruptly in rough uplands, the Heeaw Range. The Heeaws are lower than the Jedediahs, not nearly as spectacular. In fact, they can look pretty dull, but if you go there and stay a while you might be surprised. Lines of cliffs and sudden gully turns tease you in, away from sight and sound of the rest of the world. You notice that you're taking an interest, finding things. All of that country from the mighty Jedediahs eastward across town and valley and into the Heeaws, they call it the Sagehen.

The old Peterson place is the first ranch south of town, about three miles below the Conoco parking place. When he bought that property Hal Barrows, a man from Manhattan, named it "Pilgrim Ranch." A gentle mockery of his new self-image: cowman. Eight years went by. The sign over the cattle guard on the west side of the highway weathered nicely to a grey patina and the edges of the burned-in letters softened. The land behind the cattle guard looked about the same as ever and most people went on calling it the old Peterson place.

Indian summer morning, Hal Barrows' ranch yard in bright sunlight, in peace, as usual. You could think of it as too quiet, warning of deadly monotony. On certain static afternoons or grey winter mornings, John Moss, Hal Barrows' manager, might have agreed, wholeheartedly. But not today. "Should've seen it coming," he mumbled to himself. "It's come back on me again, that lack of foresight." He pressed his head and right shoulder against Dora's big body, sensed her weight shifting, her leg about to lift. He pushed harder. "Cut it out, lady." Her right hind dropped back and took weight again and milk pinged in the pail bottom, began to foam. Dora's calf, locked in her pen, complained, on and on. John switched to the other pair of teats. A car downshifted on the highway. John peeked around Dora's rear into a bright picture framed by the barn doorway: ranch house, low and modern; poplars, all in a row; hay fields, their stubble turned yellow-brown; spruce trees in dusty evergreen along the deep fold that cradled Wild Horse Creek winding out from its canyon.

The calf went suddenly quiet. No ranch dog ran barking to meet the approaching vehicle. The dog had met death on the highway, just before Christmas. The cat, on New Year's Eve, had disappeared.

Milking, caught in the ages-old rhythm, John Moss remembered the cat, tawny and sleek, a terrific mouser. From the cat he most naturally went on to thoughts of Sarah and the February morning when she had agreed that the cat wasn't coming back and she had tears in her eyes and then, her announcement. "I'm leaving, John. No more talk." She went into the bedroom, suddenly in a terrible hurry. John remembered feeding the cattle, seeing them as in a dream, hating them—and forgetting to break the overnight ice on the watering tank—and Sarah snarling at him while the two of them worked together on the pickup's cold ignition, and he snarling back. In the back porch, looking for the WD-40, he stumbled against Sarah's luggage, lined up neatly at the inner doorway. He took time out to find the fake rattlesnake. He inserted it into one of Sarah's suitcases. The snake was a soft rubber creation, amazingly realistic. No sooner had John hurried from the porch than he had second thoughts and decided to retrieve the snake, but in the hard concentration of getting the truck's motor to turn over and then driving in a ground blizzard to Goshen's two-bit airport, he forgot it.

He gave Dora's teats a final caress and stood. Usually he wiped the udder with a clean cloth, today he left cleanup to the calf. He lifted the pail, a hair's breadth ahead of another move by Dora. Once in a while she won, planted her hoof in her milk. Lately, when something like that happened, John had been apt to go into a quick rage. He'd knee Dora hard behind the ribs and punch her there, again and again. Once, he'd stomped around the barn whacking at posts and gates with a stiff hand, hurting himself, cursing. He wondered if Dora had any memory of those times. In her presence, he sometimes wondered if he felt a little bit ashamed.

A blue Taurus was in the yard. John left Dora in the stanchion. "I won't be long," he told her. "Everything's comin' to an end, lady. Just you wait."

Hal Barrows looked over his holdings: a strong corral in good repair, buildings neat and cared for, wide fields, brown hills, a long run of willows along the irrigation ditch that ran ruler straight from Wild Horse Creek. Sad, to think that all of this had once been new and exciting. He recalled his few days in the saddle, helping fetch expensive black cattle from summer range, trailing them home to his brand-new ranch. He recalled messy turmoils around shipping pens and brief camaraderie with other owners. But the landscape had remained impenetrable, the dust tiresome, the blank staring expressions on his cows' faces a continual enigma. Hal had flown east, never again did he ride the range. Instead, he paid annual visits, kept in touch by phone, trusted John Moss. Now, from a hot bucket seat, he made a final comment. "It wasn't all that much fun."

There was John, coming out of the barn's shadow, a pail in one hand, the other hand lifted in casual greeting. Hal murmured, "I hate this."

Martin
Murie

The woman in the passenger seat opened her door. "Come on, Hal, get it over with."

Hal loosened his tie and stepped out. "John, this is a hell of a thing, isn't it?" They shook hands. John looked past Hal to the woman in pale violet blouse and dark pants and small, silvery earrings. Hal said, "John, meet Lila Jaffe."

She moved gracefully, coming quickly forward with a wide, easy smile. She said, "I've heard about you." She tipped her head toward Hal. "This man is in need of legal advice. That's why I'm here."

"Well, that's nice," he said, and there was a subtle put-down in his voice and Lila didn't miss it. "I'm a lawyer," she said, "and a damned good one."

"All right," said John, and he made it sound respectful.

Hal hurried his words. "I need the money, John, and a fast settlement on another investment and if you'd like I can tell you about it."

John shook his head. "No need of that, Hal." He waited, Hal floundered, Lila intervened. "My understanding is, John, that Hal would like to offer you three months' salary, in lieu of adequate notice."

John let a little silence build. Hal, miserable, said, "Make that four months, Lila. John?"

"All right, Hal. I'll hold you to it." He smiled and hefted the milk pail. "I better take care of this."

Hal said, "Good, I'll get us a treat." He went to his car. Lila followed John into the welcome duskiness of the back porch. She felt mildly disappointed. From top to toe—dark blue baseball cap to sneakered feet—

John Moss fell short of the image Hal had painted. She conceded that John's alert, squinty brown eyes were nice. Too bad about the chin, it receded somewhat. She watched him place a filter and funnel over a gallon jar. He poured. She was caught up in the sight and sound of the smooth spill of milk.

He lifted the jar. "Want a drink? I've got some cold, in the fridge."

"I'd like that. What kind of cow?"

"Just an old Holstein. I keep her for our own use—my own use."

"Hal told me, you and your wife split up."

He was surprised she would mention that. He said, "February, a tough month."

"Yes. Tough in Manhattan too."

In the kitchen he stored the morning's milking and brought out an ugly green pitcher and poured a glassful. The car door slammed. He said, "This Sagehen country's the back end of nowhere, I guess, but Sarah loved it. She hated it, too." He tossed his cap onto a heap of newspapers and paper bags at one end of the counter. The cap had a yellow logo and letters spelling "Hagen's Trout Farm." John's hair was thin, light brown with a bare hint of white, no sideburns to speak of. "You get used to it," he said. "The country, I mean." He wished he hadn't spoken about it. No real harm, though. This woman would be flying back to the other world in a few hours. He let the hard pleasure of her presence sweep over him.

She drank some milk. "That's good," she said and ducked down slightly to look through the window at the crests of the mountains. "Is that the Jedediah Range?"

"That's the ol' Jeds. Been there forever." He ducked down next to her. The Jeds had changed, they looked almost glamorous.

She asked, "What's it like, in there?"

"Rough country. Forest Service territory. They say the hotel's to be right in front of the canyon. See that west end of the hay field? Hal's boundary line. Poor choice for a hotel, I'd say. Sun sets early, back in there. The hay grows shorter, you can notice it." He was catching from her a faint perfume. He wondered if she might be whiffing Dora's hide and hoofs and breath and his own sweat. He went to the table and sat.

Lila thought about Sarah, here at the sink, hundreds of days. She noticed gangly weeds along the near fence row. Sweet clover. She recognized them without knowing the name. The mountain skyline was a brilliant cut, signifying mystery. All that distance, wouldn't it get so that the mountains stared back at you? Children would make a difference. There hadn't been any. Hal didn't know why. And why didn't Hal know? Why hadn't he found out, somehow?

Hal came in with a pint of whiskey. He went to the fridge for ice. Lila took a chair at the table, across from John, and she said, "I noticed a couple of horses in the corral."

"Uh huh. Fat good-for-nothings."

"Don't you use them?"

"They come in handy." He gave her a slant look, teasing.

She played along. "Explain, to this city girl."

"There's some things you can do with a horse you can't do with a four-wheel drive."

"Such as?"

"Such as moving cows out of tight corners. Soon as Hal here gives the word I'll hire us a down-and-out cowpoke and he and I'll go bring in the cattle. They're still back in the draws."

"How do you feel, about horses?"

Hal gave her an angry, impatient look, but she didn't notice and John leaned toward her, elbows on the table, turning serious. "The bay gelding out there, he's one of the best all-around working horses in the whole Sagehen."

"What's his name?"

"Brownie."

She laughed, the kitchen turned dreamlike. She and Hal had been in aircraft and terminals most of the night and part of the morning. She was no longer being attentive, as John talked more about his horses, explaining that he'd bought their names right along with the rest of them. Hal had poured whiskey over ice. Lila said, "None for me, Hal, thanks. I have milk." Her voice seemed to her hoarse and distant, reminding her of the flight attendant's sleepy spiel as she wakened her passengers for the approach to Goshen airport.

She straightened and drank the rest of her milk. "Let's get to work, shall we? John, we want you to know all about this pending deal with Smoke Creek Land and Cattle Company, and you might have some suggestions. Now, Smoke Creek offers two hundred thousand for Pilgrim Ranch: land, structures, water rights. Exclusive of livestock."

John sat back, grinning. He lifted his whiskey glass. "They're putting you on. They always try. Ol' Van Horn'll do anything. This ranch is worth two-fifty, easy, at ordinary cow ranch prices. And now with Far Haven coming in, who knows? The sky's the limit."

She nodded, pleased. "There is an offer for a conservation easement, sometimes known as an open space or green space clause. Are you acquainted with that kind of thing?"

"Sure."

"The offer is tempting. Eighty thousand. It came in at the last minute, somewhat mysteriously, and that's one reason I'm here. A party in Monax, a legitimate lawyer, put the offer into legalese, all proper and correct, on behalf of another party. What do you make of this?"

"If the color of their money's good, I'd take it, and keep on raising cows."

Hal said, "I can't keep the ranch. It has to be turned into cash."

"Eighty thousand could maybe tide you over, a short while?"

Hal finished his drink and put the glass down, hard. "John, we're not talking grocery money, here. We're talking million dollar deal. Back where I work. Lower Manhattan, happens to be where I make *my* living."

"Sure, Hal. Just me having my fun."

Fun? Lila wondered. That foxy playfulness in John, might it turn cruel? Never mind, the man naturally harbored some resentments over losing a job that must have seemed more or less tenured. She said, "Boys, let's move along. What about this Vincent Van Horn? We had a preliminary round with him, all smiles, earlier this morning, in Goshen. Do you know him, John?"

"Everybody knows Vince. He's got the drugstore in town, makes most of his money in real estate."

"Tell me more."

"He was down here last week, having his look-see. I talked up the place. Vince is sharp. He's a crook, they all are."

"All who?"

"Realtors, lawyers."

"With some exceptions."

He grinned. "That's a possibility."

Hal said, "We are wondering how Van Horn might react to an easement attached to the deed."

"I suppose he'd make a big mountain out of it, use it to push the price down. You don't need me to tell you that. I'd guess Vince and Smoke Creek would figure Far Haven's lawyers can nibble away at that easement, somewhere down the road. It's Far Haven's deal, you know. Smoke Creek's just the agent."

Lila nodded. "Go for the eighty thousand, Hal?"

"Why not? I'm that much of a gambler."

John said, "Keep in mind that Smoke Creek wants this piece of land so bad they can taste it. They have *got* to have it. From what I hear, Far Haven's breathing down their neck."

x

Lila asked, "Is Far Haven a real development, not a mere S and L scam?"

"That I couldn't say, but they've sent surveyors in. Two of them spent a day up around Wild Horse. Young guys, college educated, seemed to know their business. I served them up a lunch, we had a visit."

"You're very knowledgeable," she said.

He refused the praise. "No, that was Sarah. She kept up on this sort of thing. Sarah knows about land and politics, a whole lot of things."

Lila glanced at Hal. She had gotten what she needed. Hal stood. "Listen, John, it's been a great experience for me, knowing you and watching you run this tax shelter. Hey, you did such a good job, some years we came damn close to making black ink."

John laughed dutifully at the old joke. "Well, Hal, if it hadn't been for you I'd never got to make like a rancher. Before you go, suppose you write that check."

"Check?"

"In lieu of notice."

"Oh, hell yes." He sat down and took out his checkbook and made a hurried calculation.

Lila said, "John, if you'll pardon my curiosity, where do you go from here?"

"Hard to say. First, there's those Pilgrim cattle to ship. Then I'll look around."

"I wish you luck. Nice knowing you." They shook hands. Lila went outside and waited at the car, not wanting to encumber Hal's leave-taking. She almost envied John Moss, his being cast adrift, having to "look around."

At the highway Hal stopped the car. "Do we need to check out anything in town?"

"What town?"

"Sagehen, it's just up the road a few miles."

"I'd like to see it. No, better not. We've work to do. On to Goshen."

He turned south and brought the car to a steady seventy mph. "I'm glad it's over," he said.

"It went all right. Hal, is John Moss for real?"

"He can rope and ride. Is that the question?"

"I suppose so. I mean, Adidas footwear and that awful T-cap."

Hal laughed. "Hagen's Trout Farm. Friend of his, somewhere north of Monax. Lila, if you really are dying to know, there's a straw Stetson, somewhere around the place, for summertime, like for haying. And he also owns a genuine beat-up felt model. Satisfied?"

"Thanks."

"You were intrigued, it was obvious."

"Yes." She wanted to explain that it wasn't at all what he was thinking; at least, not entirely. Instead, she sighed.

"What's the problem?" he asked.

"No problem. Oh, I don't know. Never mind, we're both so goddamn jet-lagged, it's ridiculous."

"Lila, let's think about the Sea Islands. I've been there, know my way around to some extent. What do you say?"

"Bring it up later, OK?" She watched the dry land pass by. There was nothing out there to hook onto, nothing to recognize. "Hal, would you stop the car?"

"Sure thing." He parked and she stepped out onto the road shoulder and walked to the rear where the exhaust pipe was going softly "puppa-puppa." She took a few more steps and then turned slowly to see all that there was to see. It was drab, even the distant Jedediahs had turned pale and hazy. "Earth and sky," she thought, "what more is there to be said? And if he turns off the motor, I'll go to the Sea Islands." The exhaust kept on, "puppa-puppa." She went back into the car.

Hal said, "Taking a last snapshot?"

"Something like that."

"Lila, you're in a mood. Care to share?"

"I've a funny feeling, Hal. We've barely arrived in this back end of nowhere and now we're leaving."

"So?"

"So, I was wondering what I'm missing, that's all."

"I see." He started to say more. She stopped him. "Let it rest. We have to gear down, make strategy. One more conference, if we're lucky. And I'll have to call that easement lawyer in Monax, right away. God, but I'm tired."

Chapter 6

....

 EVAN HUGHES DISCOVERED forty head of Ed Turpin's heifers on the banks of Gooch Creek, a restricted zone from which livestock were barred except during spring and fall drives. Evan phoned the TN ranch and spoke to Florence, then Ed, requesting that the animals be moved. Ed grudgingly agreed, but rang off with a threat. "You can push me only so far, Hughes. I'd advise you to bear that in mind." Evan's predecessors had had similar hassles. At BLM headquarters the Turpin file was nearly as fat as those of Abe Fox and Shawn Lynch and Lars Hamil—curmudgeons all, leaders, sagebrush rebels.

Five days later, the heifers were still there. Evan rolled down the pickup window and watched them for a while. They were up to their hocks in rich riparian muck, enjoying what was left of the amenities of Gooch Creek. One of them lifted her white face to stare. She was calm, sure of her place.

Evan drove to the TN. The ensuing shouting match had to be broken up by Florence. Evan stomped away, giving the gate a good slam-bang.

His parting words were, "Maximum fine this time. You've pushed me to it." But Florence followed him to the pickup.

"He's not well," she said. "I wish you wouldn't get him so upset."

Evan's reply was brusque. "There's one simple solution to Ed's not getting upset and you know what that is."

Later, on the road, Evan realized he'd done wrong by Florence Turpin. She was old-fashioned enough to expect from him some show of chivalry. Besides, she had no doubt been fishing for a few softer words, so that she could go back to rein in the old man. "Well, fuck all," Evan advised himself. "You are simply and most definitely not cut out for this type of work. You know that's true."

In town he picked up coffee and hamburgers to go. He drove for nearly an hour, on the east side. He pulled off the county road at the Two Creek area, still fuming. He picked up his notebook and other gear and walked up a shallow slope, looking for the iron survey stake he'd driven into the rocky ground three summers ago. He found it, easily. A shrike was using it for a perch. Maybe that was a good sign. He went to work. It was stoop labor, following the transect tape, inching along, going down on hands and knees for the hard judgment calls. His mind quit racing, out of necessity. Each brittle stem and leaf and desiccated seed head that happened to touch or overhang the tape demanded identification. He began to enjoy it. This was, after all, his thing, this messing about with habitat. He found pleasure in confirming initial assumptions, as well as in finding deviation from expectation. Sage and rabbit brush, both of low palatability, and snake weed, poisonous, were piling up high percentages along the tape, as usual. "Bare earth" was a close contender. Rice grass and winterfat made surprisingly strong showings.

He summarized the data on a standard form and added a word, "fair," to express his judgment as to the overall condition of the Two Creek range.

He went back to the truck and unbuttoned his sweaty shirt. He looked across the gullied powder-dry country. Scraggly pine and juniper held the clifflines and ridgetops, their avaricious roots spread in wide, contorted fans would keep their hold into the next century, no matter who was elected president. The ridges hazed off toward a hidden spine of the Heeaws. Evan was taking it all in, like a slow draught of bitter beer, feeling the great thirst of the country that lay open to all weathers and overgrazed by wild ungulates and half-wild cattle, stray horses, ubiquitous burros—punished by five years of drought, invaded by thistle, spiny cheatgrass, foxtail, shriveled puckers of prickly pear. He smiled, thinking about how he'd boiled it all down to one four-letter word: Fair.

He started the truck and turned it carefully, regained the road, trundled back toward town. Dust rose and settled, made its slithering attestations on glass and crackled green lacquer, like mantles of despair, if you will. But Evan willed otherwise; he was feeling good. Field work usually bucked him up, made his expertise run in high gear, forced a slow take of earth and earth's growth in forbs, grasses, brush—little changes, always—animal leavings, pocket gopher and badger workings, frost heaves, erosions. There were times when an intense patch of field work seemed like a partaking of an ancient ritual. Those were times when Evan lost most of his hostility toward the aliens, those disrupters that were poisonous or strong competitors—red danger flags to any connoisseur of rangeland. The aliens signalled disequilibrium, but under close scrutiny they became simply there—here, now—survivors, companions of the worthies, the gramas, festucas, wheat grasses whose ancestral root crowns might have been trampled by buffalo, sniffed at by wolves.

And something new turned up, always. Occasionally it would be an arrowhead, usually a locally rare plant species. Today it was a flinty red-brown pebble shaped like a bird of prey, head low and tail fanned. Eagle, say, or peregrine. Evan put it in his pocket. At home, a two-room apartment, he'd toss it into a drawer full of other pack rat treasures.

Lenore Matlock was putting things in order at the BLM reception counter. She wore a long-sleeved blouse and a cardigan because the air conditioning had been running cold, again. When Evan came in she hugged herself as a greeting. He grinned. "I'll talk to Red about it."

Lenore's answering smile was friendly. Lately she had been walking a narrow line in her job at BLM, because the impression had gotten around that she disagreed with her dad, editor of the *Sagehen Valley Courier*, accusing him of milk-toast reporting, of leaning over backward to please the cattlemen. On the other hand, she had dropped plenty of remarks about bureaucratic bungling at BLM. Which side was she on? If asked, she would have replied, "I'm just doing my job." Of course, nobody asked her. After all, short of war, Sagehen people, editors and daughters included, have to live with each other, today and tomorrow.

Evan went down the center hallway, past the rank of closed office doors. Don Sinclair's door was open. Don looked up. He looked tired. Three years short of retirement, he was working harder than ever, up to his ears in environmental impact assessments. He said, "That Turpin woman is gunning for you."

"Florence?"

"No, the daughter. Winona. Lenore handled her OK."

"Don't know what we'd do without Lenore."

"For sure, but gird up your loins. That Winona's something else, isn't she? She'll be back."

"Today?"

"So I understand."

"Thanks, Don." He went to the end of the hall and into his office. He dropped the notebook on the desk, put the transect tape on top the nearest filing cabinet. He took a comb from his pocket, but didn't have time to use it. Winona Turpin stood in the doorway. She said, "I followed you in, I heard what you and Sinclair said." She sat down and took off her hat and dropped it on the floor. Evan settled himself behind the desk and listened carefully. Winona was telling him that he had no right to take action against the TN. She passed a hand through light-brown hair that was sweaty and a little matted in places, full of shadow streaks.

Evan held up a hand. "I discussed all this, with your father and mother."

"Dad's a sick man, he's got a bad heart. I'm ramrodding the TN. I've been doing it the past year and a half and you know it."

"No, believe me, I didn't know."

"Then you don't look much where you're going, just like people say, you've got your radical head up in the clouds."

"I did not know, Winona. Really. Stupid of me, but look, Ed and I have tangled before this. He comes out the winner, every time. He's threatened me. You're aware of that?"

"Whatever it was, it's in the past. I won't have you getting him in a state."

"From now on I'll come directly to you, but the penalty stands." His hands were clasped on the desk, tightly, and she noticed. Her eyes were piercing, blue flecked with grey ice.

"Don't hand me that crap," she said. "Forty head of heifers found a break in the fence. We've been busy, and anyway we'd have gone and taken them out, first thing Saturday or Sunday."

"Is that what he told you?"

"Who? Dad?"

"Yes. It was deliberate, Winona. Your heifers went into Gooch Creek's aquatic vegetation and badly eroded banks—it's all in a precarious condition—we're trying desperately to reconstitute those kinds of—oh, hell with it." He raised his hands and let them fall limply onto the desk.

She narrowed her eyes. "You people go to extremes. Those cattle weren't doing any harm to speak of. I got them out of there, this afternoon. They're gone, OK ?"

"Yes, but they *were* doing harm. Please, I don't make these things up. And they'd still be there if I hadn't noticed them."

"That's not true."

He started to call her a liar, but held back. For a time they glared at each other. He said, "Over the years your dad's deliberately done things like this, breaking clear agreements in his lease. Political tactics is what it is, plain and simple. He and Abe Fox and the others, keeping up the pressure. Political, Winona. Everybody knows."

She slammed her fist on the desk. "We're not lawbreakers."

"Let's not get into it that way. A lot of this is not in the area of strict prosecution type procedure—negotiated agreements is mainly what we're talking about. I'm always ready for give-and-take, and your dad knows it. BLM is flexible as all hell, if the truth be known."

She picked up her hat, jammed it on her head. "I want an apology."

"You're not going to get it."

She stood and yelled at him, standard anti-government-interference doctrine. Evan crossed his arms, leaned back. She saw that he would wait her out. She shut up abruptly, and they both looked at walls, in silence, and for some reason, Winona's thoughts drifted far, back to boy-and-girl squabbles, to Leroy, sixth grader, a truck driver now, so she'd heard. He had wife and kids stationed somewhere along I 80. He and she had been wonderful loudmouths that year, and so close and so clever at disguising their affections, neither of them laying claims on the other. Leroy was a happy daredevil and had been a friendly enemy, and that's exactly what Winona wanted. Since then, nothing so sweetly combative. "Leroy," she thought, "what if you hadn't gotten pneumonia? You almost died. They shipped you down to Goshen and then your parents moved. I wonder why. You damned pest, what're you up to now? Getting a rise out of some diesel jockey? Some waitress? Funny, Leroy, how different you are from the guy I married. Brandon, smart as a whip, handsome, sexy—but a fuel hog, know what I mean? Had to have his regular gallon of TLC. If he missed out he'd turn sore, get all spavined up. I should've put a hard bit in his mouth from the first. No, a fat lot of good that would've done."

Brandon had come into the Sagehen on foot with five other travelers, on a walk for "Peace and the Earth." Each of the six gave a short speech at the elementary-school gym. Brandon had been eloquent. Winona discovered a new passion: action for a cause.

"Hell, we'll walk clear up to Alaska," she offered, but Brandon replied that his life had been turned upside down, by her.

"You're the first woman I've known who's real." She hooted at that, but forgave him.

He said, "Show me your country, show me the Sagehen." The walk for "Peace and the Earth" went on without them. Winona took Brandon to some of her secret places, but wasn't able to talk about them. He talked. Finally, it was time to make plans. Winona's mother wanted them to be married by the Mormon bishop in Goshen, but both husband and daughter reminded her that the Turpins were nothing but second-generation jack Mormons, besides which, Brandon was gentile. They settled on a civil ceremony and a huge guest list.

The newlyweds went to San Francisco. It required more than three years of California adventure to show Winona she wasn't the woman in Brandon's dream. By the time of their final showdown she'd heard the TN was in deep trouble. One foggy day she boarded a Greyhound. Many hours later she awakened to a high, hot sky and faraway nameless mountains and she couldn't wait to start over, to get down to work.

Evan, as though he had an inkling of what she was thinking, said, "You know, my family's been five generations raising cattle, in Montana. How far back do you Turpins go?"

"Just three. Well, four, counting me and my brother." She stared at him, not sure of her next move. Keeping up hostilities had always been hard for her, there was always that tendency toward play and laughter. "I'll write the check, for that penalty," she said. "I'll do it tonight. Under protest."

"Understood."

"Your family still running cows?"

"Yes."

"How come you left?"

He hesitated, then told her the truth, as he understood it. "Pride of ownership died out in me."

She repeated it, puzzled, as if she'd never heard of such a thing.

"Long story," he said. "But you wouldn't believe what a relief it was."

"So, now you're proud to be poor."

"Poor? I'm not poor. I've got a job."

She nodded, slowly. "I better go. You don't need to tell Dad I was here."

"Don't worry."

As he followed her to the doorway Evan was thinking ahead. Was this cantankerous woman going to be any less an adversary than her dad? Might she be willing to sit down and talk quietly, sometime, talk about taking thirty AUMs off her Lynx Creek lease, on a nice easy schedule? Three years, say?

And Winona was asking herself if the heifers had gone through the fence by accident. Should she ask Dad? No.

As it turned out, these musings were irrelevant. They could just as well have talked about the unusually fine fall weather or this year's hay crop or the overpopulation of deer in the Heeaws—because the TN was gone. Ed Turpin had sold it, that very day, to Far Haven by way of Smoke Creek Land and Cattle, Vincent Van Horn doing the honors. Those Gooch Creek heifers had been Ed's parting shot.

Chapter 7

MIDMORNING LULL, Jerry Haun in the pharmacy, Flora
Kimball at the front register, Vincent Van Horn at his desk
in the office. The door opened and sighed shut and Jerry
heard the tap-tap of riding boots. He looked up. Winona
Turpin, in her flat-crowned, stained workaday hat. She never wore the
hat at a cocky angle, always simply level. Jerry heard her say, to Flora,
"The ranch is sold. Far Haven's got it."

"Oh, my God!" Flora came out from behind her counter. "The TN?"

"Yes, of course the TN for Christsake, what other place would I be
talking about?"

"I didn't know," Flora said. "I didn't know a thing. He never tells
me about business." She put her arms around Winona. Jerry turned
back to his work. He heard Winona say, "Kiddo, I don't know what to
do."

The office door opened. "Jerry, could I see you a minute?"

Jerry obeyed. Van Horn shut the door. "I've got a little problem for you. The other day I was down at the Peterson place, noticed John Moss keeps a milk cow and it's got a calf. I'd like you to buy it."

"Buy... the cow?"

"No, Jerry, the calf." He chuckled. "With my money, of course. Use the pharmacy account, pay what you have to."

Jerry smoothed his hair, looked hard at the baseboard. Van Horn came forward, touched Jerry on the shoulder. "Wake up, old man. You have a hard night? Something bothering you?"

"No, I'm fine, Vince."

"Good. Me, I'm busy as hell, run off my feet. And here I'm supposed to show up in church this Sunday. So anyway, see that the calf's healthy."

"What is it, a bull calf?"

"Search me. It's black-and-white, a good looker. Flora has a thing about animals. You've probably noticed."

Jerry was puzzled. He recalled a few times when Flora had giggled over ridiculous expressions on stuffed bears, Easter bunnies, dinosaurs. He remembered a particularly wide-eyed Stegosaurus that both he and Flora had gotten a big kick out of, and Flora had said, "Jerry, you're so quiet when you laugh, a person would hardly know you're doing it."

Van Horn said, "What I'm talking about is a sort of off-the-wall wedding gift. A man my age does well to emphasize the spontaneous. That's the advice I've been getting. But you know, Jerry, I feel younger than I have for years. Being in love. I recommend it."

"Well then," Jerry said, "I'll take a look at that calf. Where should I put it?"

Van Horn cocked his head. "I hadn't thought of that." He burst into a loud laugh and Jerry did his best to join in. "Leave it with John Moss for now," Van Horn said. "Later, we'll board it some place, some nearby ranch. How about Abe Fox's place? Talk to Abe Fox, will you, get his advice. You see, I want Flora to have an entree to the country, I want her to feel free to go out any time and be with her calf, watch it grow."

Jerry smiled his thin smile, the only one he had, showing the tips of small, even teeth, but this was a moment of darkness for him. A vision stood between him and Van Horn, a vivid view of Flora, alone in a barnyard, watching a calf grow. A band tightened over Jerry's chest.

Van Horn gave a flip of his hand. "That's settled then. By the way, we had a complaint from JT."

Jerry's thumbs twitched, otherwise he kept his cool, surprising himself. His voice didn't quaver as he said, "JT seemed pleased, the other night."

"He'd damned well better've been. Next day, though, he ran into Leonard down at the Grove. You know him? Goshen S and L? Well, Leonard tells me he's sure JT came into the Grove accidentally on purpose. He sits himself down and has coffee and donut and drops a hint that the contribution this time was a bit slim."

"Slim?" Jerry forced himself to look Van Horn squarely between the eyes.

Van Horn reared back for more laughter. "You know what I told Leonard? 'Tough titty.' That's what I said. Leonard agreed, right away, and started to smooth my feathers, afraid I was taking serious offense. I'm not worried. As long as JT knows we're all doing the best we can, we'll be all right. Well, thought I'd keep you up to date."

Jerry asked, "Did anybody mention me?" And now his voice did have a quaver in it, but Van Horn didn't seem to notice. He waved a hand dismissively. "Why should anybody mention you? No, it's a tempest in a teapot. See to that calf, would you?"

"Right away, Vince."

Jerry stood quietly in the pharmacy. Here he was safe. Nobody entered the pharmacy without permission, not even Van Horn. Bottles and boxes filled two walls of metal shelving. A massive metal bench ran the length of a third wall. It held the microgram scales, the sink and glass-ware and other equipment. The front countertop supported paper pads, the phone, the computer, the *Merck Index*. Jerry stood for a long time, doing nothing, watching customers come and go. He heard Van Horn leave by the back entrance. The store became quiet, there were no customers. Flora came down the aisle to Jerry's counter. She said, "Winona asked me to go riding with her, tomorrow. I don't know if I should."

"Why not?"

"Why not go out with my best friend after my husband-to-be has just taken her ranch away?"

"Didn't you and Winona get this straightened out?"

"Straightened out? What are you talking about? Jerry, I'm not such a sweet, brainless bunny. I do know a little of what goes on. Some things you don't just straighten out with some nice words."

"Nobody calls you a brainless bunny."

"Sure they do. Everybody does, and they think I'm the big man's sweet little girl. I'm his mistress, they imagine. They're dead sure I've been sleeping with him all this time."

"Well, good Lord," Jerry said.

"Never mind, this is off the subject, which is that Winona's got nothing. She's out in the cold. Her dad showed bad judgment. I'm afraid Vince might have taken advantage—Winona thinks that, I know she does. Dammit, Jerry, maybe she's right."

"It's rough for her, Flora, but she's tough. She'll get through this."

"She's torn up by the roots. Can't you understand?"

He pressed a hand hard against his forehead, then he glanced at the office door and remembered that Vince wasn't there. He'd gone back to cruising his territory, big shark that he was, and his pet pharmacist would right away be trotting down to the Peterson place to buy a little calf be-cause the big man waved his hand and told him to go do it. "Flora, all of this is just business. We all do what we have to. Vince's job is to deal in property and if a man wants to sell, who's to say he shouldn't?"

"You haven't heard a word I've said. A man, yes, a man—does a man have a family? Does he, ever? Did you know, Ed Turpin didn't say word one to anybody? Told his wife at the last minute, when it was all a done deal." She tapped on the counter, her nicely manicured fingernails made an awful sound on the glass. "Jerry, this once, tell me what the goddamn hell you're thinking."

"Winona wouldn't lie to you, she wants you to be with her."

"So, I should go?"

"Sure. You'll kick yourself if you don't. She's your friend. Go."

She let her hands lie quietly for a few moments. She had never heard him speak with such certainty. And now he wanted to say more, she sensed it. "God," she thought, "I know him so well—and then again, I don't know him at all." She waited.

"Umm," he said, "I guess you're crazy about animals."

"What kind of question is that? Sure, I guess so. I like horses."

He sorted prescription slips. "Cats and dogs and bunnies? Dinosaurs?"

"What?"

"You go out to the TN tomorrow, Flora. Have yourself a really good day."

"Maybe I will. There's the wedding, though. In case you forgot, I am getting married day after tomorrow."

He mumbled, "How do you feel about calves?"

"What?"

"Baby cows, cute little rascals, grow up into big uglies."

She turned away and there were sudden tears in her eyes. "Oh I get it, we got a comedian here. I'm glad, makes my day." She went down the aisle to the front door where she stopped to tuck in her frilly blouse. She went out and crossed the street. Jerry looked at his watch. Quarter to twelve.

In the evening Jerry drove to his usual place, but he didn't lean on the fender, he walked through weeds, stumbled on a clump of tall purple asters. He came to the barbed wire fence and looked up at the mountains and knew that nothing was going to happen. A lone pine caught his attention. It was an outlier in front of Wild Horse, surrounded by sage. Had he seen it before? There was a brilliant bar of light at a cliff-top. Above the cliff, a long spread of talus. Talus and cliff together made the figure of a grey-blue pyramid on a golden float. The Jedediahs were hiding behind a screen of particulars. Jerry felt like walking into Wild Horse to get a handle on what had gone wrong, to wrestle with something, get back to the way things had been. But that might upset everything. But everything was already upset.

Chapter 8

···

 WHEN WINONA TURPIN returned from those years in California, the bus had dropped her off at Goshen, a block from the courthouse. The town looked dull and dry and hopeless. Winona walked the main street and she nearly cried, from pity. But Nineteen Twelve looked unchanged. She went in, hoping for a ride to Sagehen, and there sat Skip Herron, an aging cowboy, one of Abe Fox's men, tucking into a strawberry sundae. He spotted her and got up in a hurry and came to meet her.

"Winona, by God, nice to see you, what'll you have?"

"Chocolate malt."

Skip made a grand gesture, making sure a waiter had noticed. His lips were chapped, his face bony. He wore glasses now, but his outlook seemed the same as ever, alert, ready for something to go wrong. Again, Winona felt like crying. He said, "You back on a visit?"

"No, for the duration. I did my bit in the big world, the hell with it. I'm single again, Skip, and I'm glad and that's no secret."

"Me too. Lorain and me broke up, last year."

"Again? Oh, Skip! That's too bad. Any kids?"

"One." He shook his head.

"Brandon and me didn't have time. Too busy raisin' hell."

He gave her a look that meant they had a lot in common and knew each other well, and she was free and so was he. She grinned at him. "Forget it, Skip."

He laughed, pleased to have made the try.

She asked about the old ghost town. "You won't believe this," he said. "Sagehen's all set to boom." He told her about Far Haven.

Later, driving north in Skip's pickup, Winona pestered him, wanting to know everything that had happened in her absence, but he had trouble sorting the new from the not-so-new. "You get used to things, pretty soon you can't remember exactly when they came in. How about that great big neon grizzly bear on the roof of the Bear Bar?"

"That's new," she said.

He described it. "Ugliest thing in town, to my way of thinking. Now, the gold mine, that's come in since you left."

"I heard something about that."

"Way up at the north end of the Jeds. Monax gets most of the benefit. Ol' Sagehen just keeps on dyin' on the vine."

"Sagehen's been dying all my life."

"But now there's this Far Haven I told you about. That's maybe for real.."

"Good or bad?"

"Lord knows."

Winona devoted herself to the ranch, worked it toward its annual climax, the loading of bawling cattle into outward bound, manure-encrusted trucks. She learned everything all over again—machines and weather and roads, people and animals. It was a strange experience to walk into the Bear Bar and not recognize nearly everyone. Most of the strangers were miners or unemployed workers from Denver, Detroit, Houston—from all over—looking for a piece of the gold rush they'd heard about. There were a few new business people. A woman who hand-crafted jewelry and her husband who painted weird landscapes and a mechanic from Moab, Utah, owner of the new mountain bike shop. In the autumn came the hunters. There were special seasons now, for bow hunters and muzzle loaders.

And there were strangers hard to classify, some of them connected to Far Haven, most of them just passing through. The general atmosphere of the town was of people on their way to someplace else—except in the dead of winter when Sagehen returned to its ghostly quiet.

Sometimes on an evening Winona heard the rumble of a car in the long lane and she would run out to watch the headlights flash in the cottonwoods. Usually it would be Vienna Hamil and Sandra Fox. Vienna, wildcat turned into dark beauty. Sandra, nearly as coltish as ever, now a mother.

"Come on, girl, we're goin' to Goshen." And they would go, hell-for-leather, headlights reeling off fences and corner posts along County Highway 7 and State Route 11, and they knew whose fences, every one; they'd been children here, separated by miles of empty-seeming land and yet linked by that land, knowing its detail. They held to it in unspoken cunning, creatures of a hard country, and proud.

At night, in winter, the lights of the little town, frosty jewels set in mountain black, sparked across the long miles of the valley. Even when a blizzard blotted out the lights, Winona knew they were there. The town was precious at such times. Yes, it was a seedy little strip, parsimonious and failing and dull, this time of year, but to this woman recently returned from the coast those qualities were neither new nor discouraging. Like Sandra and like Vienna, Winona had known, always, that the town was a nothing place. That had been a joke, all of their lives.

But was that joke now turning on them? Was Sagehen moving on without them? They talked about it—the new Sagehen might not be theirs.

Chapter 9

 MARYA WINCHESTER gave Flora's wedding outfit a final fold and handed it to her. "My dear, I'm going to miss you, terribly."

"Don't be silly," said Flora. "I'm not going anyplace."

Marya cocked an eyebrow in disapproval. "You certainly *are* going someplace."

Later, in her room, Flora lit a cigarette and sat down at the window that overlooked a neighbor's backyard and the rise of an outside stairway that gave Flora and the other boarder a private entry. There'd been a number of advantages to living at Marya's, one being its nearness to work. The street was seven blocks long, three of them east of Main, where it ended at the grade school's playground, and four on the west, where it met open foothills of the Jedediahs. The street had no name, didn't need one, it was Sagehen's finest. The Episcopal minister and his family lived there in a turn-of-the-century house shrouded in shrubbery and trees, and the other houses, not quite as grand, sheltered in comfort a majority of the town's merchants, also a Forest Service family and two BLM families; also the doctor, a plumber, a rancher's widow, the Bluebird Cafe's owner and Jerry Haun. Jerry's house, at the extreme west end of the street, was one of the few starkly modern minimals.

Flora was sad. She watched a robin work the lawn where grass had grown sparse in the heavy shade of two big spruces. "Why hasn't that bird gone south?" she wondered. "I ought to go myself." She took in a long drag of smoke and considered once again her schedule for kicking the habit. One month after the wedding.

"I'll be in fine fettle then," she said. She crushed the butt and cried, "Oh Flora, you dumb animal!"

Marya had lied when she said she'd miss Flora. Marya knew perfectly well that she and Flora and Flora's man would be wedded to Sagehen. The three of them would be thick as thieves, in with the new breed, the developers. Far Haven technicians had been roaming the valley for weeks; they'd been seen and identified, coming and going at Van Horn's office. They were gathering data that would feed into options upon which executive boards in Denver and New York would browse. Decisions went out almost daily. A no-account cowtown was being set on a new course, its future comprehensively planned and seriously intended to rival, to surpass, Jackson Hole and Aspen, Big Sky and Park City. And it would happen in short order—that was embedded in the options—time was of the essence. Everybody expected a fast trip.

In another time and another small town, Marya Winchester had been active in community affairs and a staunch member of the LDS church. Her husband had been part owner of a heavy construction firm. Marya worked in the firm's office. After his death Marya came to Sagehen. She bought one of the old houses, fixed it up, took in boarders. She branched out as a tax consultant. Cautious and shrewd, she tested various currents, searching quite consciously for the fundamental threads of power. The search led to, among others, Vincent Van Horn. It was Marya who saw to it that Flora Kimball became a clerk at Van Horn's Rexall Drugs. Marya had taken Flora in hand, given her shelter in a hard season, but her kindness was enwrapped in a hard managerial drive. Flora had been caught between gratitude and rebellion, and she blamed herself.

Flora leaned her forehead against the cool window glass. She looked back over the past few weeks, the buildup to tomorrow's wedding. Preparations for a large public affair had begun without Flora's approval as Marya went vigorously into the project, playing her role as surrogate mother of the bride. She made delightful mountains out of each little problem, held numerous half-secret consultations with Van Horn. Flora, sidelined, watched and saw both her landlady and her fiance flaunt characteristics she'd never paid much attention to. She noticed how Marya's hazel eyes could turn from roguish joy to limpid sadness to furious admiration—in moments, flat-out. She noticed how Vince glowed, positively swelled, under heavy doses of flattery. Flora shrugged it off, she even teased Vince about it. Now, on the day before the wedding, she tried to coax up a shiver of jealousy, and felt nothing. "I'll go to Winona's," she decided. She looked at her watch. It came as a shock that there was plenty of time. Absolutely everything had been taken care of, by Marya. Flora took her jacket and car keys and slipped down the outside stairs. "I'm getting out," she thought.

At the TN, she parked in spotty shade of cottonwoods. Half of their yellow leaves were scattered across the yard. Flora took a deep expectant breath, this was a place where time slowed, like stepping into a huge eddy. It didn't last long, today; angry voices were sounding inside the house and a door slammed. A man came clattering down the back porch steps. He stomped across the yard to a footbridge over an irrigation ditch, his boots thumped on the boards. A woman waited for him in front of a neat, white house where four young poplars grew in a straight line at the edge of a tiny lawn. The woman's pose was stiff, her arms akimbo. She and the man consulted each other, apparently in full agreement.

More thumps of boots, and there was Winona, on the long, screened front porch of the old ranch house. "You came! Let's go, I got the horses in the barn." They ran across grass and crinkly cottonwood leaves, into the barn, into sharp aromas of hay, new and old, and fresh manure, well-kept leather, dusty cobwebs.

Winona said, "I bridled them. Hoped you'd be along." She pointed to a taffy-colored horse. "Snuffy, you know him. I got this goddamn stallion." She picked up a saddle blanket and reached for the bridle of a tall-shouldered black beast who stood stiff-legged, his eyes shifty. Winona spoke to him, gently cursing his attitude. She flipped the blanket onto his back. He shivered his hide. She said, "His name's Naughty. He's looking for an excuse."

"Why bother with a stallion?"

"He's mine, as of yesterday. I've got to try him out."

"Really? He's yours?"

"I know, it's crazy." She went to the saddle rack, indicated Snuffy's saddle. But Flora was still entranced by Naughty. "God, how insulted he looks—I wouldn't climb on him, not for a million dollars."

"Yes, you would."

They rode down the long lane under cottonwood shadows. Naughty pranced; Winona had her hands full. At County 7, Naughty broke free in a hard gallop, north. Flora held Snuffy to a trot and felt abandoned. The valley had never seemed so wide.

"All right, Snuffy. Cheer me up." She tapped her heels just twice on his belly and he loped away. Flora clamped into his rhythm, a wild sureness took her, the memories were still there in mind and legs and shoulders, horse clatter and creak of leather. The valley blurred, wind tore at her hair, her breath whipped.

Winona turned Naughty off the road and onto a steep truck track that had become an erosion channel cut through tall sage. The rough going brought the stallion to a quick walk. Winona made him stop and they waited until Snuffy caught up. The stallion looked over his shoulder. Snuffy snorted. Both horses stood quietly, rich autumn sunlight bright on their hides.

"How's Snuffy today? If you had the chance, would you buy him?"

"I'm no judge, you know that."

"You know how to ride."

"Go ahead with your stallion, don't let me hold you back."

"Hey! You thought I was showing off."

Flora shrugged. "Doesn't matter. I'm sorry, kiddo. I'm in a terrible mood."

"Good, we can keep each other company. Anyway, the truth is, it was nip and tuck with Naughty, back there. The best way was to give him his head."

Flora nodded. "Why'd you get stuck with him?"

"Bought him yesterday. Paid a good price. I'll sell him, later. Everything will have to be sold. I bought Naughty because I was feeling guilty and Art didn't want to keep him any longer."

"Who is Art?"

"Oh, sorry. He's all-around cowboy, comes from real buckaroo country. He and Sharon have only been with us a year. They were just getting settled at the TN and Sharon's expecting and then Dad up and sells the place. Naturally, Art and Sharon are as pissed as any of us. They're left high and dry and winter coming on."

"He should realize it's not your fault."

"Later, when the air clears. Right now neither of them can see facts. They see injustice. The final blowup came today. I guess you saw the tail end of it. I can't stand much more of this."

"He's a good-looking man."

"And knows it, but so what? He and Sharon are solid folks." She put Naughty into a walk. The day turned hot. Winona noticed a coyote track in dust, but Flora wasn't interested.

Winona asked, "Where'd you learn to ride?"

"In Twin Falls, I had a best friend. I was a townie and she rode the school bus, nearly an hour every day. Sometimes I'd get on the bus and go home with her and we'd have us a country weekend. Her family ran a truck farm, but they kept two horses. I rode Irma's brother's horse. Those were great times. I guess those were about the best."

Winona pointed to the head of the draw where a few mountain maples had turned fiery scarlet. "Yes," Flora said, in such a forlorn voice that Winona reined in and gave her a hard look.

"Tomorrow," Flora said.

"Don't I know it? I'll be there in a town gown. You won't know me."

"I'll probably break down and cry. You know something? I'm one of these women too weak to be much good out in the tooth-and-claw world—and Vince is good to me, he spoils me, and I like it. I go for it. I'm about to settle for it."

Winona laughed. "Flora, you kill me sometimes. You're square in the middle of tooth-and-claw, right where the action is. Don't you know it?"

"I live in that drugstore, nothing much happens. It's safe. Don't you see what I'm trying to say?"

"I'm not sure—maybe I do."

"I need that security, can't stand to be alone. I've got a lousy personality."

Winona didn't want to go round and round on "personality." She'd had enough of that in the past few years. "What was it like with *Walker's Wanderers?*"

"We hardly ever had enough money, that was what it was like." Winona waited, Flora squinted upwards toward the mountain maples, remembering. "In some ways we were free as birds. We lived in motels mostly, and nobody knew where we were. And nobody gave a damn."

"How long did you and Walker stick it out?"

"Almost five years. It wasn't all bad."

"I always thought a country-and-western combo would be about as glamorous as you can get."

"There was some glamor. And for a while the guys even thought I could improve myself and get to be the female vocalist. My voice was OK, but personality-wise I was hopeless. They said, 'Flora, you're the greatest, we all love you, but you've got to learn to project.'"

"Oh boy, doesn't that make a person feel about 5 years old? Tell me about the glamor."

Flora laughed. "Well, Reno was always the best gig, and as high as we ever got. There's two or three little spots there, off the main drag. Reno still had some nice things about it, if you knew where to go. And then, Cheyenne. You won't believe this, we had a ball in Cheyenne. Right in the middle of winter."

"You saw a lot of country."

"Main drags of little towns, mostly. And we never made it to the coast."

"Brandon and me did the coast. San Diego to Arcata. You name it, we did it. Made money, spent it, got in trouble. Some of it was glorious, out of this world. Man, you ought to see some of those great beaches. There's still some places where you have to walk to get to—you come out on the biggest sky in the world, just ocean and shore. And surf, humongous surf roaring away, not giving one hoot in hell whether you're there or not. We had us some good times, Brandon and me, we really did."

The trail petered out in a jam of whitebark pine and up-angled ridge rock. They dismounted and sat in the shade. The DuckWing Ranch was a tiny hyphen in the south and the TN looked like a collection of neat toys: house, barn, sheds, corral, two square patches of lawn, garden square, trees. Further west, the irrigation ditches made precise lines across hayfields. Meadows meandered between low hummocks of sage. A tiny streak of silver was the sky reflected in a slow curve of the Sagehen River.

Winona said, "I bet this is the last time I'll ever be up here."

"What will you do?"

"Get a job downtown? I don't know. I haven't the faintest idea."

"The TN was on hard times, but you'd have liked to go down with some fight."

"No. I wasn't planning on going down. The Turpins have been in the Sagehen for a long time. Things might have been different if Ken had stayed. Dad counted on Ken. Now he treats him like a traitor. And me, I'm just his beloved daughter."

"He's a veterinarian, isn't he? In Missoula? What's so wrong about that?"

"Dad always assumed the TN would go the usual way: father to son, but Ken told him no, he liked being a vet. Besides, his wife is a town girl, didn't want to be stuck on a ranch. Well, I took over, bit by bit. Dad kept working, after the heart attack. The doctor kept warning him. I never sided with the doctor, but Mom did. It was really me in charge."

"I saw your dad go into the office with Vince, but I didn't think about it. I've got no interest in real estate. I don't know what all goes on in that office."

"Flora, will you for Christsake quit harping on what you saw and what you didn't know? None of this has got anything to do with you and me."

For a while they listened to the horses grazing. Flora said, "Have you talked to Sandra and Vienna?"

"Not yet. I'm scared to."

"You ought to."

"I know. I will. See that big willow patch down toward the DuckWing? We'd go swimming there, us kids. There's a diversion dam. Sometimes there'd be a dozen of us, Ken and me and two or three of the Hamil tribe and the Prestons and Dillard Fox, and Sandra. And there was always some kids belonging to a haying crew family or an irrigator's family. Some of the kids we never really got to know, they came and went. But Lordy, the fun we had—naked as jaybirds—mud fights—swiped each other's clothes. Learned a thing or two down there. I remember Dillard—oh well, that's between him and me. I still go down to the river if it's a hot day and mosquitoes not too bad. I take everything off and jump in and float. It's like being a muskrat. You're low in the water, watching the banks go by."

She got up and went to the horses. Her voice had broken and her eyes were wet and she was mad at her weakness. She checked Naughty's cinch and then Snuffy's.

Flora asked, "What should I do?"

"About what?"

"Tomorrow."

"You so nervous you can't stand it?"

"Yes, but that's not it. I have doubts."

"Uh-oh. Well, if it's any comfort, so have I. John Moss wants him and me to ride off into the sunset. Weird, isn't it, everything coming down all at once?"

"How long's this been going on?"

"A while, in a sort of easygoing way, but last night it got serious. I had to tell him it would be nice to go on being friends."

"That won't work."

"Won't it? Well, what else could I do? I respect the guy, I trust him, I think. It's just that, oh you know—and he's over forty."

"If we're talking age, I'm twenty-seven and the man I'm meeting at the altar tomorrow is exactly twice that."

"That's different. You told me yourself, you don't plan on babies."

"You and John could have babies. You're making excuses. Don't do that. Be realistic. Oh, I'm a great one to be giving out advice."

"You're right, though, I suppose. I married Brandon in a cloud of romance. Hard to believe that it lasted so long."

"The romance bit."

"Amazing, isn't it? Then the mist cleared. I'm down to earth now, for good."

Flora smiled into the distance. "I see through you, kiddo. You're waiting for it to happen again."

"No, not that way."

"Yes, that way. You're dying for lightning to strike twice."

They came out of the hills by way of a cattle driveway, a wide grassy draw marked by sun-baked hoof prints. A fat woodchuck stood up from its grazing, then made a rush for the nearest burrow. There was the excuse Naughty had been looking for. He spooked and nearly tossed his rider, but she managed to keep her seat and forced him into a high-stepping, head-tossing trot. She turned him, slowly, toward where Flora had dismounted. The woodchuck had disappeared. Flora found the burrow entrance. She went down on hands and knees to get a near look at the dark, animal-smelling hole. Winona's shadow fell across her. "You oughtn't to let Snuffy's reins trail."

"Oh, right."

Winona sat down, then stretched out and looked into the sky. Flora said, "About tomorrow, I've been thinking. Could you come to town early and go with me to John Moss's?"

"If you're trying to patch me and John together, forget it."

"Nothing to do with you. Vince is giving me a calf—don't ask me why, please—Jerry told me. My God, you'd have laughed to see Jerry, he acted like he'd stolen the crown jewels, told me he'd been the one to buy the calf, said Vince put him up to it, said Vince claimed he was too busy, and it was supposed to be a secret. Well, Jerry was acting so strange mumbling away about me being crazy about animals. Later on, I figured something weird was going on. I went back and cornered Jerry and made him spill the secret. I just now decided, tomorrow I'll give John Moss a call, make an appointment, go down there and look at my calf."

"Flora, are you making this up?"

"I'll find out, tomorrow."

Winona sat up. She picked a stem of saltbush and broke it into tiny pieces. "OK, I can face John Moss."

"Wear pants. Get dressed up later, at my place."

"Yes, sir! What time?"

"Around ten?"

"That's cutting it sort of fine, isn't it? Wedding's set for two, right?"

"Marya's taking care of every last thing. Plenty of time."

"I'll leave the car with Mom and Dad, catch a ride with Sandra. It's time I talked with Sandra, heart-to-heart."

They lay there for a while, the horses disturbed the ground, clumping along, heads down, grazing. The woodchuck put his head carefully into the sunlit part of his burrow entrance and froze, listening, barely breathing, his eyes round, black, shiny. Nobody noticed.

Flora said, "You sure John Moss is out of the question?"

Winona didn't answer; she felt guilty, she'd been thinking about Evan Hughes. Strange man, obsessed with "saving the range."

Flora sighed. "What if lightning never does strike? What's a woman to do?"

Flora's car, coughing and jerking, barely made it to Will's Garage. Will said it looked like a fuel line problem, but if it was the carburator, he'd have to get one of those electronic modules from Napa in Goshen. "Monday afternoon, maybe."

"OK," Flora said and she was thinking, "Maybe it's an omen. No, maybe a nudge."

Chapter 10

 SUNDAY MORNING, bright sky. Jerry Haun gave Flora and Winona a lift to the Peterson place. Flora insisted he drop them at the cattle guard. He said, "I can just as well run you on in," and he slowed to make the turn. Flora shouted, "Stop, I mean it. It's not even a quarter mile. I want to walk." He stopped and they got out.

They walked in silence, their low-heeled street shoes sounding faintly on the dusty gravel road. Hay fields were quiet, blackbirds had flown. Flora wore an imitation straw sun hat and they both carried jackets.

John saw them coming. He waited in the yard. He'd taken a bath and washed his hair. He gave Flora a complicit grin. "Come on in, look over your livestock."

"So, it's real, is it?"

"Come see."

At the barn doorway John stood aside and when Winona passed him he said, "How you doing?"

"Fine. You?"

He nodded. Flora murmured, "Why, you cute little devil." The calf stood spraddle-legged, staring at them, one of its eyes obscured, surrounded by black fur, the other eye glaring from a patch of pure white. Dora had her head in alfalfa, tossing and chewing, paying nobody any mind. The calf moved her head in sudden jerks, questioning the world. She did a frisky sidestep, stopped on a dime, posed still as a statue. She was at her glossy, limpid-eyed best, the peak of calfhood. Flora leaned over the top board of the calf's pen, but for a while she didn't reach out.

John recognized the restraint of one who had never had a richness of choices. "Flora's lovely," he thought. "Why Van Horn? Well, I'll tell you; the answer is: none of your business." But John Moss always took self-cautionings with a grain of salt, and now, with this funniness, this calf wedding present thing, he was tempted to make it his business. However, he had a more personal problem—Winona. He took to watching her, couldn't keep from it even as he tried a hard-eyed, no-nonsense judgment gaze: ordinary ranch woman, waist nowhere near waspy, wide mouth, round shoulders. And she could be ornery, stubborn as a fence post. He'd known her since the time he and Sarah first came into the Sagehen. Eight years. Only in the past several months had he become stricken.

She gave him a sideward glance and the helplessness came back; he fell into the old round of self-pity. Damn! Hair-triggered quirk at the corner of that mouth and readiness in those eyes. Sometimes John had the conceit to believe no one else noticed the impish quicksilver in Winona's eyes. At other times, a vision came over him: Winona staring into another man, giving him one of those blue-grey gazes, scrambling his wits.

He went into the heat of the yard and stomped into the house. He sat down at the corner table, took the checkbook from the drawer, studied the record. With Hal's check added in, the near future looked more than tolerable. He tore out a deposit slip and began a list of assets: One pickup, poor. One black gelding, fair. One bay gelding, ex. Saddle gear, OK.

He got up and wandered through the rooms. Favorite chair, leave it. Clothes, pick out the best, leave the rest. Rifle, keep it. At the front window he stopped to look through the lace curtains and he wondered why Sarah had left those with him. Heirlooms, she'd told him, on that first day when she'd hung them in their new home. He hadn't asked why or what or where. There had been a lot of things he never asked about. Was that important? He noticed how quiet the room was. He didn't often come in here in the middle of the day.

He went into the kitchen and ran water into the coffee pot, then noticed the wall clock showing a quarter to twelve. He stepped into the front porch. Winona was pacing up and down in front of the barn, her thumbs hooked in her belt.

John called to her. "Gettin' on toward noon."

She came to the porch and spoke through the screen. "Flora just now told me Jerry's not supposed to come back for us. Can you beat that? How did she think we'd get back to town? What's going on?"

"I can give you guys a lift to town."

"Yeah, well, let me go talk to Flora."

John watched her go. He recalled a time when weddings always had to have some foolery tied into them. It was expected—something more than throwing rice. He went to the pickup and cleared some junk mail and empty feed sacks from the cab. He was still thinking about weddings, one in particular where horseplay had gotten out of hand, starting as a simple bride-stealing stunt and, somehow or other, stretching out to well past midnight, coming close to bad hands-on stuff, a bunch of drunk cowboys passing the point of anything that could be called judgment.

John shook his head. The memories lingered. He lifted the hood of the truck and disconnected three sparkplugs. He closed the hood as quietly as possible.

Winona and Flora came from the barn, Flora with her hands in her pockets, walking as though in a dream. Winona looked at John, shrugged, climbed into the cab. Flora followed her. The cab was hot as a pistol. John ground the starter, the motor coughed, gave up. He kept on trying until the smell of flooding became rich. He stepped out and lifted the hood to make the usual motions. He noticed Flora climbing out of the cab. She walked slowly across the yard. Suddenly, Winona was next to him, her close-cropped hair fluffed forward to graze the rim of the air cleaner. Her eyes lighted. "Well, no wonder." She showed him a dangling ignition cable, then she paused, stared at three naked sparkplug tips. She held the boot of one cable just above one of the plugs. "Number one?" He didn't answer. His shoulder was hard against hers and hers didn't yield. They both rested there on the warm metal of the motor well.

"Winona, goddammit, why'd you have to happen?"

She waited long enough to let him know she'd heard and was giving it some consideration, then she stepped away from him. "Never mind that. You tell me what's with this vehicle."

He kicked at the ground.

She said, "Well, OK. We'll play it that way. How about your phone?"

They glanced at each other, looking ahead, making plans. He said, "That's a funny thing, Winona, phone's on the blink."

"Uh huh. That is so funny, being that Flora phoned you just this morning." They looked down the length of the yard to where Flora leaned on the top rail of the corral, watching the horses, smoking.

John said, "Sorry I busted out at you."

She said, "It's one tough ol' world, John. Don't think I don't know it."

Flora came back to them, stripping her cigarette, concentrating fiercely. Winona told her about the truck and the phone, both dead. Flora nodded, said nothing. The calf squealed.

"Calf's hungry," John said. "What about her, Flora? What do you want me to do with her?"

"Oh ... keep her.... I don't know ... I'm all confused."

Winona was losing her nerve and so was John. He said, "I better saddle the horses."

At a few minutes past noon the women rode out in the direction of Wild Horse Canyon, to pick up the west-side trail to town. John watched them go. The silence of the ranch yard was like a heavy pressure.

Chapter 11

....

 AFTER LUNCH, John reconnected the ignition cables. The motor turned over at the first try. John drove south on Route 11, then east on Fox Road and crossed the river above the old Spring Gulch ford. The sky had begun to haze over; it looked like rain. The road ran between Fox's OX on the south and the recently defunct DuckWing on the north. At County 7 he went north, passed the DuckWing, the TN, the Mule Bit. At the Hagerstroms' gate he turned onto a washboard gravel track. The meadows here had never been plowed; their yield of natural hay was known throughout the Sagehen, ranked close to alfalfa in nutritional value, but the Hagerstroms didn't have enough bottomland, so they had to buy extra hay every winter to carry their animals through.

Wes Hagerstrom came from the house, crossing the yard like a man sleepwalking. He had a palsy; lately he'd begun to have trouble speaking; some claimed it was Parkinsons, but Wes wasn't saying. He had no sons, his daughters were married. A daughter and son-in-law, Julie and Garth, ran the place. Wes said, "Garth's out after some steers got through the fence. I don't expect him till suppertime."

"You suppose he'd have time to give me a hand, like last year?"

"I think he would." Wes was speaking with care, standing upright, desperate to keep his voice steady.

John said, "My last roundup, guess you heard."

"I feel bad about that, John."

"Tell Garth it'll be worth a little more to him, this time. We'll have us a last fling." He put his forearms on the gate post to show he'd stay for a while. They discussed the usual things, worked into the usual abstractions—prices, weather, war, government. John was surprised at the vehemence with which Wes attacked the new gold mine. He began to stammer badly, had to pause, and John waited. Wes said, "Men will do anything for gold." His failing voice gave the old saying a fresh doomsday sound.

John was wondering why we all keep bitching about things we always have with us and can't do anything about. He lost track of Wes's words, his thoughts went to somewhere in Manhattan. Papers on desks, computer screens, spiffy receptionist—black cattle, prize Angus stock, shimmering, turning into sheaves of paper—paper flamed into scatters of gold. The images pleased him.

Wes kept his gaze steadily on his visitor, as if that would tame the alien that made him stammer. John thought, "I could just as well stand here till supper time, keep the old man company. Nobody would know the difference, except Dora. He studied the road and its cottonwood border and the willows that had spread from the creek to the very edge of a big weed patch where Grace Hagerstrom, when she ruled here, had kept a big garden. A window curtain flicked. That would be Julie, checking on Wes, but holding back.

A good half hour passed before John took his leave. He drove farther north to an asphalt crossroad. Now his thoughts were far to the south, the Peterson place—Pilgrim Ranch. He saw himself as though from a great distance—a small figure going in and out of the barn, in and out of the house, the sheds, the corral. Shoveling snow, breaking ice. Hauling wood, cutting hay. In and out, in and out. He smiled, tapped the steering wheel. It was all over. It all fell away—the responsibility, the careful husbanding of another man's resources. Gone. He was a free man, and it had been, after all, a fluke, a marrying-the-boss's-daughter type of thing, not likely to be repeated. He rolled down the window, stuck his elbow out, hummed along. The warm autumn breeze went with this new devil-may-care up-lift and that went with the solid rumbling of the truck.

At age sixteen John Moss had gone out from a Colorado feedlot town to prove he was a cowboy. He'd proved it, but only after hitting rock bottom, taking misery to his bosom. Working for wages was something you couldn't pass on to somebody else. You learned to take it. Simple. He entertained old scenes—a cow camp, cattle kicking up manure dust, grit in everybody's teeth, the riders seldom speaking, stiff in the saddle like dried-up rag dolls—night coming on, nothing going quite right. First order of business: animals. Feed, water, pickets, hobbles—and don't think they'll ever thank you for it.

He was back on State 11, headed south, the View Motel shining bright blue like a welcome at the town's north edge. He drove into Sagehen's Sunday hush. A gathering of young males lounged at Will's Garage, propped against vehicles, watching each other and the street, fondling soft drinks. Long hair and short hair, Stetsons and T-caps, town and country, these were some of the folks not invited to the wedding.

He parked at the dead end of a side street, three blocks off Main. Behind a small house was a shed and a tiny, rough pasture. The house was 1930s style: grey stucco, steep roof, rosebushes along one side, twinberry honeysuckle at the front porch, lilac at the picket gate. John heard the sounds of an axe biting wood. He walked down a side path. Red Izard glanced up, went back to his work of pointing fence posts. He was hatless, his russet top hair hung over his forehead. He gave a final lick to a post, tossed it aside. He straightened slowly, easing his back, grunted at John. He pulled a pack of cigarettes from a pocket, offered it.

"I quit," said John.

"That's right, you did." He lit up and shook the match as if he couldn't douse it fast enough. "I hear Evan Hughes is putting sheep on your range."

John shrugged. Red sat down on his chopping block. "Look at me," he said, "doing company work on Sunday." He was in charge of maintenance at the BLM District Office; his responsibilities included a half acre of fenced-in heavy equipment, lawn, borders, indoor facilities, the flag and the flag pole. "You wait," he said. "A man of your experience can find something good with that Far Haven outfit. They'll need guys like you to herd the dudes around, saddle their horses." He laughed. "You've got the figure for it. So, it's come down to sheep in the Sagehen."

"Might not be the first time."

"Oh? This is cow country, so I've been led to understand."

"Cowmen always say that, but I've known cases where some will switch from cows to sheep and back again, depending on markets. Sheepmen the same. You got my horses?"

"Wish I did. You selling Brownie?"

"Brownie? Go on!"

"So, what're we talking about."

"Winona Turpin and Flora Kimball rode up from my place. I told them to leave the horses with you."

"First I've heard of it."

"That's funny. You suppose they tied up at Marya's?"

"Could be. Let's go see. Belle's down at the church, watching, like a lot of other nosy people."

They started walking toward Main Street. A blue Chevy sedan passed the intersection, jerked to a stop, backed and came toward them. Red said, "Uh oh." The car stopped and Marya Winchester heaved herself to the passenger side and rolled down the window. She was a picture: grey hair blue-rinsed to match silver earrings and a dress the color of harebells. She said, "I just got back from your place. Where are the girls?"

"Borrowed my horses to ride back to town. My truck wouldn't start."

She was quick. "I see. Then how did you get to town, John?"

He tipped his head toward Red's house. "That's my pickup, I got it started." He began to explain, but she waved a hand, impatiently, bracelets jangled. "What the devil was Flora doing down at your place, on her wedding day?"

"That's what I was about to tell you." He began again and got as far as the selling of the calf to Jerry Haun. Marya broke in. "You and Jerry have no right to be fooling around like that —on a woman's wedding day— whatever possessed you?"

John stooped down, put a hand on the door frame. "Marya, listen to me. It was Van Horn. Listen to what I'm saying to you. Hell, I didn't even want to sell my calf. I asked a price you wouldn't believe. Jerry met it. Anyway, the point is, the last I saw of Winona and Flora they were riding across my west hayfield."

"There are two horses standing in your corral," she said. "I saw them. I went through your house, John. The barn, everywhere."

"Why my place, Marya ?"

"I got it out of Jerry, that he'd driven them down there. Now you listen to me. There are a bay and a black in your corral. The whole place is quiet as a grave." She put a hand to her mouth, her eyes opened wide. "Get in, we'll go to the church."

John stood back, speechless. Red leaned into the window. "You go ahead, Marya. We'll walk."

By now the town was in mountain shadow. Most of the onlookers and a few of the wedding guests were considering going home, but when Marya drove up, people clustered around to watch her and George Wadham discuss the situation. Wadham and two sons owned Valley Hardware, one of the town's most venerable enterprises. Sylvester Matlock, the *Courier's* owner and editor, stood near Wadham, an ancient Speed Graphic hung around his neck. Matlock had been hired to take the wedding pictures. What he was to take, instead, on this day, would make the *Courier's* front page. Citizens would save that page, fold it and tuck it into scrapbooks.

By the time Red Izard and John Moss ambled onto the scene, Marya had dispatched a messenger to Vincent Van Horn's residence, only two blocks away, and she and old Wadham had come to some terrifying conclusions.

"John Moss," she called, "come here."

John and Red stepped onto the drought-stricken lawn of the Church of Saint John in the Wilderness and stopped in front of Marya. Her hands were folded at her waist, she stood erect, buxom and formidable. "John, you tell me that Flora and Winona took your horses, but those horses are in your corral. I saw them, less than an hour ago. You tell me that Jerry Haun drove the girls down there, but he never came back for them. You tell me that Flora went clear down to your place, on the morning of her wedding, to look at a calf. You say that calf was a gift, a wedding gift."

She paused, to catch her breath. John said, "Jerry Haun bought that damned calf. I told you. Where the hell is Jerry? He can straighten this all out in a jiffy." He looked beyond Marya, saw fixed expressions on faces of friends and acquaintances. They were waiting, every one of them, and their massive silence was the likes of something John Moss had never been required to endure.

Marya resumed. "I heard what you claimed, you don't have to keep speaking of it. You also claimed your truck wouldn't start, but this very minute, that truck is here in town, in front of Red Izard's house."

Red said, "Hold on there, Marya, let's not go off on a big stampede here."

George Wadham took two quick steps, poked Red on the chest, using two stiff fingers. "Let her finish," he said His pale eyes were like marbles.

Red whispered, "Jesus."

John shouted, "Get hold of Jerry Haun."

At last, movement in the crowd, but no one found Jerry Haun. And now people were shifting to make a space for Vincent Van Horn. He stepped into it, his aura of authority so strong it was like an aromatic mist. He said, "All right, John Moss, what do you have to say?"

John's anger had taken root. "I'm sick of talking about this. Nobody's listened to a word I say." He faced away from Van Horn, spoke to Wadham. "Tell him I've got no idea where Flora went. Tell him I'm through with these damn questions."

Van Horn raised his voice. "John Moss, what have you done?"

Marya murmured, "Something awful." She touched Van Horn, leaned against him, and the minister came from his seclusion in the vestry Everyone stood in respectful silence, but nothing came of it. The minister, a tall, thin man, stooped down to Marya, spoke to her alone. Afterwards, there was much discussion as to the exact nature of the consolation, or admonition, he had administered.

George Wadham took charge. "Let's do this right," he said. "Make up two parties. One makes a sweep south from here, along the west-side trail. The other one drives down to the Peterson place, check that out, work north from there."

Someone asked, "What about Wild Horse Canyon?"

Wadham replied, "Later. We got to be systematic in this. Anybody need good headlamps, come to the store." He turned to his middle-aged son. "Herman, go unlock." Herman hurried away.

Red Izard said, "I've got a horse," and John Moss said, "Ride down the west-side trail. That's probably where they're at."

Wadham nodded approval, but Van Horn clapped a hand on John's shoulder. "And you're not going anywhere."

"Huh? What're you talking about?"

"No time for argument, John Moss. We are obliged to hold you here—under lock and key."

"Lock and key—you're crazy!"

Wadham nudged a man next to him, the mayor, a jovial figurehead. Wadham told him to "go get Bagley." The mayor shouldered his way to the street.

Van Horn announced, "I hereby make a citizen arrest."

John said, "You can't do that—who the hell you think you are?"

Van Horn ignored that, raised his eyebrows at Wadham. "George?"

Red nudged John. "I'll get on that trail, we'll get this thing straightened out in a goddamn hurry." He went away at a fast dogtrot. He wanted to help his friend, but he also loved action.

John stood alone. He saw something he had thought happened only in movies: fellow citizens making little facing-away motions, backing from him, shuffling, actually taking little quarter steps, edging away. It was dumb, it was something to laugh at, but a mist enveloped him, his neck was hot, he went for Van Horn with a hard insult-slap on the side of the face, and then another. Van Horn was quick, John took a sharp flare of pain in his ribs. He and Van Horn closed, punching and shoving. Van Horn backed off to begin a clumsy weaving, but John didn't want that, the kind of fight that petered out in some kind of face-saving standoff. He wanted to punish Van Horn, he wanted to hear him howl. He rushed him.

At last, Sagehen citizens shed some of their abject passivity. They couldn't stand there like dummies and watch an elderly leading citizen indulge in a punch-out, especially on his wedding day, especially with a man they'd just finished wrapping in guilt black and terrible. They moved into the fray. John was lifted and dragged. The town roared in his ears, roof-lines tipped in the sky above the sharp smell of trampled grass. Two men had iron grips on his arms. He quit struggling, the mist cleared. He was hemmed in by faces, they were close and oppressive. There was Ed Turpin, his mouth grim, the rest of his expression shaded by his hat, and Florence Turpin, her eyes full of dread. And now John felt it. Dread. What had happened to those women?

A fuel tanker barreled down Main Street, followed by two cars. John looked that way. He thought, "They're just passing through, don't know about this little spot of crazy hell." But one of the cars slowed and turned and John recognized it. One of Sagehen's two police cruisers, Fred Bagley at the wheel, the mayor with him. The cruiser drifted to the curb and Fred heaved himself out. He looked sleepy. He left his hat in the car, also his gun. He grinned, showing small, jagged teeth, his eyes twinkled. "What seems to be the matter?"

Chapter 12

 WHEN BELLE IZARD saw her husband leave the church she followed him, but at her own pace. She was delayed by a neighbor who wanted to know what had happened. At the front door of her house she paused, feeling uncomfortable about John Moss's pickup parked there. What would people think? She liked John Moss, but she had her family to think of, so she told herself. She walked down the side path to the shed at the back of the lot. She watched Red. He was saddling Dan. He glanced at her and didn't like the amused tolerance act she was putting on. Dan's head was up, his ears pricked toward the darkening wide world outside his cramped quarters.

Belle said, "Good boy, Dan. Here's your chance to earn your keep. Go be a hero." Red gave her a look. She said, "Push him hard, Red."

He reached to a spike that held his off-duty Stetson and a thigh-length coat. He put on the hat, ramming it down angrily. He lashed the coat behind the saddle. "What a way to talk," he said. "This could be a serious situation."

"I know it. I'm wondering what we should do about John's pickup."

He swung aboard, then peered down at her, questioning silently, understanding her. "Leave it for now."

"You call, soon as you know something."

"Sure." He held Dan to a walk to the street. The horse was as eager as his rider to get out of there, hit the trail, cover ground. Belle watched them clatter into the street. She noticed dark clouds piling up in the west, shot through with sunset color.

"All right," she decided. "No laundry tomorrow. I'll pick up a pal and go to Goshen, spend a half day in a real town. Spend some money, have a banana split." The phone was ringing. She bounded up the back porch steps. The top tread shifted and she had to do a quick two-step to catch her balance. When would Red get around to it? Maintenance man, hah! Her mouth was stern as she lifted the receiver.

"This is Fred Bagley, down at the station?"

"If you want Red," she said, "he just rode out."

"I guess I missed him then."

"Looks like it."

"Reason I called, John Moss here, he's worried about that milk cow of his. The cow's got to be milked. I was thinking Red might do it so long as he's down that way."

"I'm sorry, he's out of reach, for now."

"I've been coordinating things here, busy as a one-armed paper hanger—having one heck of a time finding somebody can milk a cow— you'd think in a town like Sagehen...."

"Yes," Belle said, "I understand—I suppose Henry could do it."

"Who?"

"Henry, my son."

"Oh, sure. Well, could he do that? I'd be much obliged."

"And what about John's pickup? It's here, at our house. It shouldn't be left here."

"You think it shouldn't..." Bagley's voice trailed off as he considered yet another problem. "I should think we could leave it be, for now, Mrs. Izard."

"Belle. For godsake, Fred, call me Belle. I'd rather the pickup was some-place else."

"Tell you what, Belle, have Henry stop in here. I'll give him the keys, he can drive it down there and back, leave it at the station."

"Good. Thank you, Fred." She hung up and laughed at herself. Why was she sending Henry, when she was the family's best milker and gen-eral all-around cow manager? She found Henry in the living room.

"Get your feet off the couch."

He looked up from his paperback, *High Country Drifters,* and frowned. He put his feet down. She looked at him, thoughtfully, as though consid-ering whether he was worth keeping. Her dark eyes were intent, her pep-per-and-salt hair a tangle. It occurred to Henry that she was beautiful. His mother, beautiful.

She said, "I guess you don't know what happened, at the church."

"Yeah, I do. Wedding. Ol' Van Horn and that young..."

"Stop, listen to me." She told him that John Moss had been arrested, and why. Then she relayed Fred Bagley's request.

Henry was taking an interest. "So, ol' Bagley wants me to drive down there and..."

"Fred Bagley is barely 50 years old, and you're to milk the cow and come right back. Take your coat, it's going to rain."

From under the long awning that fronted the half-block length of the Yarbidge Building, Linder Schlegel peered into the rainy dark, listening intently to a shouted argument inside the Town Offices complex, two doors to the south. Linder could easily imagine the scene, lighted by a single desk lamp, Fred Bagley at the desk, John Moss in the cell, about six yards back. Linder had a casual acquaintance with Fred, a man so accepting of people and the world's doings that he was nearly unbelievable—and Howie, his partner, handsome and restless and with a mean streak. The two men had in common their growing up in cattle ranch families, from which they had run, at the first opportunity, to the nearest town. Both could, however, turn sentimental about land and families. JT Timberlake's *Free Range* was one of the publications usually present in the pileup of papers on their desk.

Linder tilted against the old brick wall. He was a bearded, youngish man, overweight, dressed casually, but not sloppily. His bentwood chair had been supplied by himself. Whenever he quitted his accustomed observation post in public space under the Yarbidge awning, he took the chair with him into what had been the lobby of the Yarbidge House, once Sagehen's finest, and only, hotel. The lobby, thirty-five feet square, was currently the display room of Sagebrush Faction, where tourists found oil paintings on the walls and jewelry made of stone, metal and hardwood displayed in glass-topped cases. Linder heard footsteps on the street. "A youth," he said. "Ought to know him— name's on the tip of my tongue. Ah—got it." He called out, "Henry Izard, what brings you out on this dark and dreary night?"

Henry stopped at the edge of the awning. "I've got to go milk John Moss's cow."

"Now, that's the first sensible thing I've heard all day. Come in out of the weather."

Henry obeyed. Linder said, "I'll lay you ten to one, Citizen Henry, that John Moss is innocent. He is guilty of thoughts, naturally. We all are. Fantastically guilty, every last one of us miserable dogs." He waited, a teasing smile on his broad face. Henry shrugged. Linder wouldn't let up. "Come on, Citizen, wouldn't you have to agree?"

Henry said, "I don't know John Moss very well."

"All right, be evasive, be of the crowd." Linder was no longer smiling.

Henry felt guilty. Linder sighed and said, "Never mind. I've been sitting here listening to John's shouts. He's outraged, mad as a hornet. Tone of voice, manner of speech, those are clues."

"Yeah," Henry said, "that's important."

A woman appeared in the shaft of light thrown by the open doorway of Sagebrush Faction. "My wife," Linder said.

She wore a pale yellow blouse and jeans and moccasins. As heavy-bodied as her mate, she moved with grace, making scarcely a sound.

"Who's this?" she asked.

"Beth, meet Henry Izard."

"Hi," said Henry.

She smiled. "Don't let this man lead you astray, Henry. He thinks he's got the town all figured out, snared in a net of words."

"Not true, Lightfoot," said Linder, "not true."

She put a hand on Linder's shoulder, absently. "Henry, don't feel bad if you find Sagehen confusing. You do, don't you? Especially on a night like this?" She waited, smiling.

Henry looked up from the splintery sidewalk. "Yeah, it's confusing," he said.

Beth went to the dripping edge of the awning, held her hand out, to catch drops.

Henry said, "I better get going."

She said, "You take care."

The interior of the barn was lighted by a row of four bulbs, but no one was there. Henry took note of the stanchions, the pens, the hay bales, the cow and calf. He guessed that the milk pail would be at the house, and it was, on the drainboard at the sink in the back porch. The ranch yard was full of vehicles. Flashlights and headlamps blinked and flared in the distance.

Henry led the cow to the nearest stanchion. She wore a thick, heavy wreath made of chokecherry branches woven together and decorated with freshly picked flowers. There were spikes of goldenrod, their colors rich in the barn's light; stiff sprigs of paintbrush, scarlet edged with green; purple asters and tufty yellow-headed plants that Henry didn't know the names of. He hunkered down to knead the udder and was pleased that the teats were large and graspable, unlike the family cow back in Utah.

The Izards had started keeping a cow and a horse as soon as Red's job with Utah BLM became secure. The job had begun as a temporary stint of stoop labor on an archeological survey of Anasazi cultural sites. Red's restless energy had annoyed some of his fellow workers. He had an abrupt kind of eagerness and a perfectionism that never faltered, no matter how bad the heat, or dull the drudgery. The foreman remarked that "the red-head thinks this is all a big adventure and saving the world and I don't know what all—pain in the butt." Red stayed with the BLM. A few years later came the transfer to Sagehen, and a family crisis, Belle balking at adjustment to another dusty dog of a town. She wanted a taste of urban life, for herself, for the boys.

"Not big city," she said, "just a decent town."

"Sagehen's a town," Red countered. "We'll live right in it. What more do you want? Besides, what the hell choice do we have?"

"I want more than population eight hundred."

"It's a lot more than that in summer."

It was the first time they'd fought hard in front of the boys. Brent backed his father. Henry, the younger, sided with his mother, weighing in with tantrums and bad language. Red won. When they made the move the two brothers rode in the back of the pickup, keeping an eye on Dan who followed behind in a homemade horse trailer.

Milk rattled in the pail, Henry was dreaming. Dora lifted a hind foot, plunked it into the pail. "Shit," Henry said. He gave her a shove and she moved her foot, tipping the pail. Henry grabbed the pail in time and went on with the milking. He left some for the calf. He led the cow back to her pen and heaped hay in her manger. He turned the calf loose and it scooted to the udder. Henry closed the gate and turned out the lights. He dumped the milk in weeds just outside the door.

Headlights were sweeping the yard, illuminating wet figures of men and boys. Henry began to identify individual voices, some of them kids his age and older. He'd be seeing them soon, on the bus, third week of school. He heard his dad's voice, saw him ease his lanky frame into somebody's car. The Ponera County sheriff, Pierre Labray, ambled here and there, speaking softly. A state patrol cruiser nosed in and the trooper conferred briefly with Labray. Cars were sorting themselves out, getting under way. From the shouting and loud talk, Henry easily gathered that the search was being called off, to resume first thing in the morning.

Where was Dan? Henry jogged to the corral. Dan stood under a shelter at the far end of the corral, with two other horses. Henry put his back against the corral poles, watched the last vehicle leave. In the dark, wet turmoil, nobody had paid any attention to John's pickup. A fresh spatter of rain came at Henry and he put up the hood of his coat and walked back to the truck and stopped to stare at the barn, remembering what Linder Schlegel had said.

"I'll lay you ten to one...."

Henry's young mind raced among facts of the day and the night; when he remembered the wreath around the cow's neck, his thoughts slowed and circled. He couldn't imagine John Moss spending time making up such a big flowery thing. Well, of course, the women had done it. When did they do it? Hah! There was the question. Step by step, Henry built his theory and was ready to side with Citizen Schlegel.

"Ten to one," he said. "Good enough." And it was as though he had suddenly taken a big step into the world.

Chapter 13

BETH AND LINDER SCHLEGEL had switched off the TV, but they didn't go to bed. Beth made some decaf. They sat on the couch, one at each end, under reading lamps, a book, unopened, on each lap. The search parties had returned, wet and cranky and with no findings. The rain had eased. Beth said, "I've phoned Jerry three times, that's enough. We might as well face it."

"Just what is it we might be facing?"

"Don't pretend. Jerry Haun was seen driving out of Sagehen, this morning. The two women were with him. None of them have been seen since."

"Fact. And, face this: Jerry is about the most repressed character we have met in our long and checkered career."

"Careers, dear."

"Correction noted. Also, Jerry is a friend. I'd say that, wouldn't you?"

"He's never paid much attention to me, one way or another. He does sit quietly when you carry on about painting. The best listener you've ever had. But, yes, I feel secure around him—and friendly. Even now, even tonight, I say that."

"You have it a little twisted, Lightfoot, about my jabberings on art. Jerry puts in a word, now and again."

"I hadn't noticed. Linder, did you ever consider the possibility that he finds Sagebrush Faction merely a convenient, non-demanding place in which to get away from the store—take his lunch break?"

"That's obvious enough. So what?"

"Nothing."

They sipped their decaf. The rain started again. Beth said, "I don't feel creepy around Jerry. At first, I did. Do you understand that?"

"Do I have to?"

She went to a window and pulled a curtain aside, saw her reflection in dark glass. "He's been traumatized—somewhere, somehow. Women, I suppose. Or men?"

"What does that tell us? We're all pretty well fucked up by the age of ten. Is that a knock? Yes, the street door." Linder went into the hallway, opened an inside doorway and crossed the cavernous display lobby. He opened a heavy, antique door and faced Jerry Haun, who took a step back, onto the sidewalk. "Linder, I'm worried sick about Flora."

"And Winona? What about Winona? Jerry, do you know something we don't?" Linder was blocking the doorway.

Jerry ducked his head awkwardly, turned, looked along the street. "I've been all over, drove down to Goshen, up to Monax."

"Since about what time, Jerry?" Linder had come down to basics, making himself deaf to his own inquisitorial tone.

"Marya called me, sometime before noon. She was upset, said Flora had been acting strange."

"And had she?"

"Flora? Umm, yes, I think so. Linder, something's happened.... I can't stop driving around ... can't go home ... saw your light was on."

Then Beth was there, shoving past Linder. "Jerry, for godsake get in here. I'll get you a drink. We'll talk. *You* will talk."

Fred Bagley looked up from his magazine. "Hi, Henry. Everything go OK?"

"Yeah. I found something kind of interesting."

John Moss banged on the bars. His cage was just beyond the single spill of light from the lamp over Fred's desk. He said, "Henry, speak up."

Bagley leaned back, put his magazine down.

Henry said, raising his voice a little, "A big wreath, hanging around the cow's neck."

Fred began to grin, but the stolid look on Henry's face stopped him. This kid was trying awfully hard. "A wreath," he said. "Like for Christmas."

"Yes, but really huge. And it's fresh, got flowers in it, hardly wilted at all."

Bagley glanced into the dimness at the back of the room. "John, this mean anything to you?"

"Not a thing. Let me out of here, I'll find those two for you. Goddammit, Fred, use your head. Quit cow-towing to Van Horn."

"Hush, John. We've been over all that." He turned to Henry. "Well, where is this thing?"

"Outside, in the pickup."

"Why'n't you bring it in here?"

"Didn't know if you'd be interested." He sounded sulky.

Fred pushed his chair back. "All right, let's go have a look. You know, I ought to have impounded that truck."

"Impounded?"

"Forensic evidence."

John yelled, "You go to hell, Fred!"

Bagley continued. "Now you've gone and put fingerprints all over—well, not your fault, Henry. Never mind, this'll all sort out in the morning." He went to the door and down the one step to the sidewalk. John hissed, "Henry, please—keys in the desk drawer, right hand. Come on, man, how about it? I know how to find the women and nobody's listening."

Henry stood stock still, between the desk and the door, caught like a dumb donkey, but a demon voice came out of the strange night, out of the past. "Here is your test."

He found himself at the desk, the drawer open, keys in his hand. Cool metal. Touch of power. A pang of fear and joy took him. What he did now would make a difference.

John called to him, his voice hoarse. "The biggest key, Henry."

The big key worked like magic, the door swung, bumping hard against Henry. John, sneaker-footed, moved like a big shadowy cat, disappeared into the maze of halls and rooms of the Yarbidge Building. Henry closed the cell door and scooted to the desk, dropped the keys into the drawer. Three big bounds and he was on the sidewalk, off-balance, staggering toward Fred Bagley whose arms were full of aromatic herbs. "It is a big one," Bagley said. "I don't know what to make of it. Thanks, anyway, Henry." He heaved himself into the Town Offices. "Henry, you go on home now. I'll hang onto this. Thanks for your help."

"OK." Henry ran across the street to where he'd parked the pickup. He hid there, peered across the hood, waited for Bagley's alarm and outrage. "I better get the hell out," he whispered, but curiosity held him there. He wanted to see the result of his exploit. And, he still had the keys to the pickup.

Nothing happened. Henry forced a long slow breath. "What's Bagley doing in there?" A shadow moved across the lighted Venetian blinds of the Town Offices. There was nothing frantic about it. Another shadow moved on the white wall of the Bluebird Cafc. John Moss. The only sounds were the pat-pat of his running and the gentle drips of rainwater from eaves, the town was that quiet. Once again, the rain had slackened, to a fine mist. Henry jumped into the pickup, fired it, made a U-turn and drove past John and stopped. John piled in, breathing so hard he couldn't speak. Henry turned on the headlights and drove south. The road was wet and not in the best of condition. Henry stayed at a sensible sixty mph. John asked, "What's this about a wreath?"

"Chokecherry, and flowers. A lot of paintbrush. Those would have come from over by Wild Horse, I figured."

"They sure as hell would. What else did you figure?"

"Winona and Flora came back to your place, to put that wreath on the cow. Why, I don't know. That means they didn't ride up the west-side trail. They unsaddled your horses and went somewhere."

"I could have made that wreath, Henry. I could have put the horses in the corral. That's what everybody thinks."

"Yes, but you didn't."

"I didn't?"

"Wouldn't have made sense for you to tell everybody Flora and Winona had the horses, if all the time you knew the horses were in the corral, for anybody to see."

"By God, yes! For any busybody, like Marya Winchester."

"Forensic evidence."

John laughed. "Now why didn't I think up all that? Why didn't some-body at the church slow down and work this out?"

"Too busy, I guess. I don't know. How about Flora and Winona? You think they're OK?"

"I about went crazy, back there in jail, thinking up all the things that might have gone wrong. But I know, now, where to look. Henry, I'm much obliged to you. It took quick nerve back there, to break me out. Drop me off at my place and drive this truck back to town, park it, play dumb. That's the only advice I can think of."

Henry turned into John's driveway and coaxed the pickup along the mud and gravel mess left by the search parties. He said, "I'll help you go look."

"No, you're in deep enough as it is."

Henry didn't answer that. He parked the pickup at the house and followed John into the kitchen. John switched on the light. "Not bad," he said. "They only broke one cup and used up half the coffee and left a sink full of dishes." He opened a drawer, found a large baggie, poured coffee into it. "I'll take this along. Can't live without coffee. Henry, you clear out now. I'll take all the blame I can, for what happened back there. Don't you worry."

Henry gripped a chair back, leaned on it hard, stared at the floor. "You're going on a search."

"Damned right I am, and I'll find those two."

"Count me in."

"No, and thanks again. I won't forget what you've done for me."

Henry's lips were on the verge of setting into a sulky cramp. He fought it off. "John, I got a right." He raised his head.

John, beginning to speak, hesitated. He leaned back against the sink and crossed his arms and thought about justice. Henry had gone way out on a limb. Henry had done some powerful detective work. And there was the pesky fact of Henry being fifteen, sixteen, thereabouts. These all entailed rights, of one sort or another. He said, "There's two pairs of saddlebags in the shed by the corral. Look to the left of the tractor as you go in. We'll need both sets."

Henry nodded, unable to speak. When he returned with the saddlebags he asked, "Where we going?"

"On a gamble. South, to the next town."

"Blackrock."

"Yes, we'll call that a town. I've a notion that whatever went down, here today, it has to do with Flora getting cold feet. Trying to put myself in her shoes, I picked up something reckless—a kind of sneaking out from under kind of thing—like getting myself to the nearest bus depot."

"And Winona went along with it."

"Oh my yes, that Winona, she's the type to go along with anything the least bit harebrained."

Chapter 14

LATE MORNING, south of the Jedediahs, the air dry and hot, horizons indistinct. Henry had spent the night on pine duff, under a single blanket and a slicker. Once, he woke to the sounds of rain drip and horses on picket lines. He had seen a star dancing in high pine branches, and fallen asleep. Now, on the black horse named Jug, riding toward Blackrock, Henry was suffering from thirst and weariness and he had a crick in the neck, but a determination to measure up was still with him. That, and curiosity.

A jackrabbit loped away, disturbing pristine rivulets of fine sand laid dawn by last night's storm. Jug plodded on, unstartled. Henry bent low over the saddle to study surfaces that lay open to the sky, waiting new passages. He saw what looked like scamper marks of a kangaroo rat. The painstaking tracking had gone on since dawn, with no results. Rain had wiped out yesterday's records.

A coyote appeared, seemingly out of nowhere. It bounded at an oblique angle, keeping one eye on Henry and Jug. Again, Jug took the sudden sight in stride. Henry appreciated the horse's tranquil approach to the world. He shaded his eyes to watch the coyote, and caught sight of another motion—directly ahead, toward Blackrock. He squinted hard into the haze. The figure broke into two, became again one. Henry shouted, "John!" He chopped at the air, indicating direction. John acknowledged with a lifted hand and Brownie leaped into a flowing lope. Jug noticed, he stepped lively, Henry gave him his head. Under Jug's sleek black hide were still-youthful muscles, but he couldn't gain on Brownie. Brownie was no ordinary horse. By the time Jug caught up, a happy confab was taking place, Winona and Flora and John standing together on Brownie's shady side.

Henry heard Winona telling about the wreath. "It was a beauty, John. We made it for you, left it on Dora—showing off, that's all. Didn't you like it?"

Henry swung down. "You should've left a message," he blurted. Flora recognized his nervous eagerness. Her heart went out to him. "I know," she said, "but we didn't have the time, and I didn't have the guts to go back to town and face up to—whatever."

Winona snorted. "Drop that, Flora. We've gone back and forth on that, we've trampled all over it. So, Henry, John, you going to give us the true picture?"

Henry grinned and pointed to John. The story came out, in short phrases interrupted by cries of incredulity, from the women. Henry noticed that John was leaving out big chunks. "Just as well," he thought, "and let's get a move on."

Flora said, "John, can I bum a cigarette?"

He shook his head. "I quit, only last month. Pure hell. I know how you feel." He started walking, leading Brownie, and Jug followed. "Let's get on to Blackrock," John said. "Say, how come you didn't use my phone, let somebody know...?"

"Your phone was out of order, remember?" She burst into happy laughter.

"Winona explained about that, did she?"

"Yes."

"Sorry, Flora. I shouldn't have played that on you."

"No, I'm glad you did. The big mistake, yesterday, was us unsaddling the horses. We could have ridden to Blackrock. Actually, the problem was me, I kept procrastinating, wouldn't stick to one plan more than five minutes. Right, Winona?"

Winona agreed, but added, "The really huge disaster was Marya Winchester. I was in your house, about to phone my folks, let them in on what Flora was up to—swear them to secrecy—and here comes Marya. Lucky I recognized her car, barely had time to swipe some food from your kitchen and sneak out the back way."

"That woman," said Flora, "she went through the barn and house, everywhere. We had to hide in the irrigation ditch. I couldn't stand it. I crawled down the ditch and got in a patch of willows and lit out."

They crested a rise and there was Blackrock, teasing them, appearing so near, but the tamarisks that shielded the buildings looked tiny. John issued a caution. "A good long mile yet to go."

They plodded on. John and Flora and Brownie. Henry and Winona and Jug. Winona had noticed the rifle riding in Brownie's saddle boot, and the bulging saddle bags and the bedroll tied behind the cantle. And John was rigged out in boots and his old Stetson. Jobless, technically a fugitive, he was on the move. Flora was running, too. She'd be out of the county by nightfall. Henry, he'd head for more prosperous country in a couple of years, as soon as he finished high school. And Winona? Two weeks to go before Smoke Creek took formal possession of the TN. Then Winona'd be tempted to light out for some other territory. She laughed— that was her way, there had to be a laugh, always—but this one was short, bitter.

Henry looked at her and, because he walked in a thirsty dream where many things were permissible, his left eyebrow went up, a sophisticated question mark.

She said, "I was thinking, only coyotes and pack rats will hang on in the Sagehen."

"I know it," he said.

She wished he hadn't agreed so quickly.

Blackrock began as a homestead. The ranching operation failed, but the family held on, converted to selling gas and groceries to stockmen, truckers, miners, old-time prospectors, corporate and federal geologists, and the first wave of Easterners who were touring the West to find the best last of it. Blackrock now consists of a restaurant and garage, with associated outbuildings and mobile homes on both sides of Route 11, four miles south of the Jedediahs. On the restaurant's letterhead you find a small coyote, on the left, howling, and this: "Ma Grenville's. Gateway to the Sagehen. Finest Western Cuisine." The restaurant has tamarisks on its north and south flanks. The east side is the highway frontage. In back, a rocky gully winds to a greasewood jungle, a place that had been a big, busy corral made of juniper posts set double so that sagebrush bundles could be packed between them to make thick walls. The corral had been part of a hopeful, ambitious enterprise, and women and men and dogs and horses had themselves some times. South of Blackrock is nothing but miles of bleak desert, all the way to Goshen.

Geraldine Grenville presided from behind the cash register, paying half a mind to the low clicks and hums of satisfied clientele. One more day of success. Geraldine had a reputation and she basked in it and was a little bit bored. She watched four new arrivals. A scruffy lot, they were hitching two horses to the ornamental iron fence that Geraldine had put up recently as a protection for her long, narrow strip of front lawn. The four customers came into the newly-refurbished entryway where framed scenes of mountain meadows, horses and cowpunchers hung on knotty-pine walls. The woman in the lead gave Geraldine a big smile and strode to the counter. "You've dolled up the place, I can still smell the varnish."

"Winona Turpin, where in God's name—we've been worried sick."

"Everything's fine and dandy, but I better call my folks."

Geraldine waved her to her phone. "And then you can tell me all about it."

"Don't rush me, Geraldine. Do you know Flora Kimball?"

"I do now. Hello, Flora."

Winona turned abruptly to the phone, leaving Flora to do her own fielding. Flora said, "I'd like to buy a pack of cigarettes."

John and Henry were hanging back, pretending to study the pictures. Geraldine laid the cigarettes on the counter, made change, noticed Flora's trembling. A heavy smoker herself, Geraldine was ready with her lighter and as she leaned close, she asked, "Are you all right?"

Flora made the effort, raised her voice. "I'm very well, thank you. Decided not to get married, that's all." She took a long drag of smoke, let it out slowly. She met Geraldine's gaze, said, "John Moss had a lot of bad treatment, all because of me."

Geraldine came out from behind her counter.

John said, "Morning, Geraldine."

"It's way past noon," she said. "Who's your partner?"

"Henry Izard."

She looked hard at Henry. "Well, as long as everybody's safe, that's all I care. You must be starved." She led them to a table. Skillful and brisk, she guided Flora to the chair facing the window, summoned a waitress and went away. Winona was still hunched over the phone.

Flora and John and Henry, their knees tucked under heavy linen, waited in embarrassed silence while the waitress served iced water. They drank. The waitress poured coffee, refilled the glasses. Flora said, "Henry, you ought to call up your mom and dad."

"Sure, if Winona ever gets off the phone."

"Tell them I'm sorry."

John wagged a finger in front of her. "That'll be enough of 'sorry.' You got to shake the habit, Flora. We're all in on this. Isn't that right, Henry."

Henry put both forearms on the table, leaning toward Flora, pleased as punch. "That's right, Flora."

John was watching Henry, a smile crept across his face. Flora noticed. She said, "I'm glad something is amusing." She put out her cigarette. The fresh coffee was sending a lazy aroma across the table. John spread his arms, laughing. Flora laughed. She caught Henry's eye. Somehow, Henry knew what it was all about and he joined in. "Damn," he was thinking, "this is living."

Chapter 15

FLORENCE TURPIN put down the phone and cried for a few moments, then she called Belle Izard and gave her the good news. Belle agreed to call Marya Winchester, and Marya called Van Horn.

At the Peterson place, Sheriff Pierre Labray happened to be in the kitchen making coffee when the phone rang. He answered and listened intently to Vincent Van Horn's bad-mouthing of John Moss, his insisting that some weird conspiracy was still underway. "You'd better get down to Blackrock," he said. Labray scowled. Through the lace curtains of John Moss's living room he saw Red Izard ride into the yard, long-faced, slumped in the saddle, returned from another fruitless foray. Labray hung up on Van Horn and ran out of the house. "Red, Henry's OK." The smile on Red's face made all the trouble of the past eighteen hours worthwhile.

Red stepped down from Dan. Labray checked his watch. Would they still be serving lunch at Ma's? He looked west into the field where his deputy, Bull Hogan, and a line of searchers were nearly done with the irrigation ditches. Labray gave them a drawn out "Yi-eep, yi-eep," waved them in. "Red, you come with me. Leave the horse, let's get on down there."

At Blackrock, the sheriff parked next to two horses that were snubbed up to the iron fence. Red jumped out, strode toward the restaurant entrance, but he paused, noticing that Labray had approached Brownie. Red said, "You ever see that horse before?"

"No. I've heard about him."

"You look him over."

Labray did that. He put his shoulder against Brownie and leaned down to slide a firm hand grip along Brownie's left front leg. He stood back to survey the barrel, the haunches, the spine. He took hold of the bridle and looked into Brownie's lazy, deceptive eyes. Two more vehicles had swooped from the highway. From one came Vincent Van Horn, from the other, Ed Turpin. In another moment, Bull Hogan arrived, parking the cruiser gently, smiling at his boss. He waited for Labray to quit his obsessive judging of horseflesh. Bull's face was bland and beefy, his gimlet eyes quiet, noticing things, like the way Ed Turpin and Vincent Van Horn pretended the other wasn't there.

A crowd had gathered, from nowhere, it seemed. Van Horn called out, "Flora." Then the action started: Winona rushing out to bear hug her father, Red Izard pushing rudely past Van Horn, Flora trying to sidle past everyone, to gain the street. Van Horn opened his arms wide, embraced Flora. She murmured, "No, Vince, wait, please." He wouldn't let go, he turned her and started to walk her to his car. She screamed, "No, Vince, let me go!" John Moss came leaping out of the restaurant to drop a heavy hand on Van Horn's shoulder and Van Horn turned, growling, aching to get at the dirty animal who'd stolen his woman, but Sheriff Labray grabbed Van Horn from behind, and Bull Hogan nonchalantly put his big body in front of John.

Van Horn looked around wildly, found Flora and changed his tune. Speaking softly, he said, "Flora, you and I—we have some things to talk over— privately." She shook her head, staring at him through tears. He advanced upon her.

Ed Turpin shouted, "Hold it, Van Horn," and in a quieter voice, "Flora is welcome at the ranch. Friend of my daughter, she'll stay as long as she likes."

Flora looked at Ed, whom she hardly knew, and he took her silence for consent. He offered his arm, she accepted. They walked to the Turpins' car. Winona gawked. "Perfect, Pa," she decided, "but damned if it isn't just like you—gracious old range master—making all the decisions." She felt a grief that had no name; it was for him, it was for she knew not what.

Van Horn exploded. "The ranch you say? What ranch, Ed Turpin? I bought it, you damned fool."

Ed gave him a thin smile. "According to the contract, Smoke Creek takes possession in two week's time. Until such time I advise you not to set one foot on any part of the TN." He turned away.

Everyone heard Van Horn's bitter words: "Dumb has-been."

They didn't bother Ed Turpin, not much. There were lots worse ways of going out.

The sheriff noticed that John Moss had slipped along the fence and was untying Brownie's reins, and Henry Izard was backing toward the black horse. Labray said, "Wait, John, we've business to settle."

"What business is that, sheriff?" John stepped into the saddle and Brownie backed and danced onto the asphalt of the highway like the skilled roping horse that he was.

Labray said, "Quit clowning, John. You broke jail. That's got to be dealt with."

Henry fit a foot to Jug's stirrup. Van Horn said, "By God, Pierre, if you don't arrest that man I'll do it myself."

John sneered, gave a hard tug on his hat brim, looked down at Van Horn, and anger slammed through him and humiliating scenes from the lawn in front of St John in the Wilderness swam across his vision. Not again, no way. He turned Brownie. Before everyone's eyes, horse and rider disappeared, in the tamarisk hedge on the east side of the highway, leaving only a discreet shimmering of dusty green branches.

Red Izard was watching Henry. Would Henry do it? Would this secretive, lazy son— this strange one—?

Henry did it, put heels to Jug. Pierre Labray made a grab for the bridle, missing by a hair. Jug broke stride on the asphalt, but he recovered and made it through the hedge.

Bull Hogan dived into his cruiser and came out with a rifle. Red Izard yelled, "No you don't, that's my son." Red realized, too late, that Bull intended only a warning shot—too late to hold back his own long, low football tackle that took Bull and the rifle into a bruising sprawl against the iron fence. The rifle barked.

The crowd froze. No one spoke. Pierre Labray broke the silence. "Anybody hurt?"

Winona said, "I'm pretty sure it was up in the air."

Labray let out a long sigh, and spoke. "All right, that's enough foolishness. Everybody clear out. It's over." He pointed at Van Horn, wordlessly, then at Ed Turpin.

Bull came up to Labray, said, "I caught a sight of Brownie's dust, Pierre—they're headed for goddamn Tunbridge Wells."

"Oh, that's just lovely, Bull. We'll need horses."

"I know it."

Chapter 16

....

HENRY WATCHED ONE of the sheriff's cruisers speed south on Highway 11. Brownie, far ahead, held steadily in the same direction, roughly parallel to the highway. That seemed a dumb way to go. What was John up to? Jug plodded into a gully and the gully deepened gradually to become a miniature dirt canyon. Heat hammered from the walls. Occasional clumps of mesquite cast mere laceworks of shade. Henry had no hat, his head hummed. He hunched over the saddle and closed his eyes. "Made the wrong move," he thought. The table at Ma Grenville's, ice water, camaraderie—those marked the place where he should have dropped out.

The walls lowered, ran out as gritty spits into an alkali flat that glared like hot silver. In the distance a tropical island floated on blue. Jug moved with confidence into the alkali. Henry slitted his eyes. Several minutes passed before he noticed that Jug was following a trail—Brownie's. Each of Brownie's hoof steps had thrown up bits of dirty-white crust. Each bit cast a late afternoon shadow. The trail was curving now, onto a gravelly slope. Jug never faltered, sometimes he broke into a jerky trot. Now he was traveling north by east, the terrain level to rolling, the vegetation so sparse that each clump of prickly pear and each pincushion tuft of herbage looked like an item of decor placed with careful forethought on the pebbly ground. A tall jackrabbit sat erect, motionless, waiting for Jug to pass by. The southern fringe of the Sagehen appeared, Jedediahs on the left and outliers of the Heeaws on the right, the valley a mere supposition between them. Jug's steps quickened. Directly ahead, a hazy slash of autumn gold—willow or cottonwood. Two buildings, low and weathered grey; there would be water. After a while, Henry could hear it, the gurgle and splash of water.

Jug crossed turfy ground to a battered stock tank into which a beautiful strand of water fell from an iron pipe half-clogged with rust and golden and green algae. Algae slimed the tank's surface. Jug thrust his muzzle into it. Henry slipped down, gathered in cupped hands from the pipe's lavish outflow. He drank. He sloshed water over his face and let water drip where it would and drank again. God, how delicious! He stood still, studying details: corral, house, barn—all polished, brittle and worn. He marveled at Jug's drinking, its loudness, and it seemed to Henry that everything was announcing itself—tilt of roofless barn, smell of ancient manure, stare of the house windows, cottonwoods clean against sky, an enamel kitchen pot, chipped raggedy blue and rust and white, half buried in barnyard duff. Shock of standing on earth. Wine of water. A swallow flitted across the face of the barn.

The house stood whopper-jawed on slightly higher ground. In spite of all the signs of abandonment, the windows were intact. Henry knew that a corporation ran cattle over a huge range that stretched from Tunbridge Wells to the Heeaws and an Air Force low-level flight area. This old has-been building might be one of their line camps.

Jug whinnied. An answer came from behind the house. Jug tugged that way and Henry went with him. On a patchy green pasture, Brownie grazed, untethered. Near a small, nearly smokeless campfire, John Moss sat, on a rickety kitchen chair, his hands clasped behind his head. From under his hat brim he looked at Henry.

"Turn Jug loose," he said. "He'll stick with Brownie." Henry looped the reins back and came to the fire. Jug ambled toward Brownie, muzzle down. John asked, "What happened back there? I heard a shot."

"I don't know."

"Had me worried."

"Yeah." He poked at a few partly burned twigs of sage, and they lofted wisps of white ash. John picked up a stick and hooked it under the handle of a big tin cup that was sitting on coals, steaming. He pulled it away from the fire.

Henry said, "You got time for this?"

"Always time for coffee. Join me."

"Sure." Henry didn't like coffee, but he'd try it again. He sat on his heels, got ready for what John would say next. Henry, no dummy, knew he'd had one foot in real drama and another in misty desire: to be a "High Country Drifter." That was an uncomfortable part of why he'd climbed onto Jug and ridden out of Blackrock.

John said, "How do you figure Red will take this?"

"Won't like it."

"He's a good man, your dad. Except I know damn-all about dads." He laughed. "I'm no authority, understand?"

"Sure."

"Mine died when I was eight. Where's your brother now? I forget his name."

"Brent. He's a wrangler, way over in the Wind Rivers. He's tough, takes no shit from anybody."

"Don't worry, chances are he'll get over it."

Henry looked across the fire. "Get over what?"

"You heard me."

Henry worked on that. John said, "I take it Brent is like his dad, horse crazy."

"I'll say!"

"And you're not."

Henry shrugged. John said, "Jug is not what you'd call a real comfy ride. Did he bolt with you, back there?"

"I almost fell off, going through those tamarisks. No, Jug was good. He's steady."

"He is. He's jerky-gaited, takes some getting used to, but ol' Jug's a damned reliable horse."

"I grabbed the saddle horn," Henry said. "Both hands."

"I should hope to Betsy you did. That's what it's there for." He lifted the coffee cup to his lips, tested cautiously.

"It's for dallying a rope around."

"Where'd you get that from, Brent?"

"I guess."

"Henry, Brent has some things to learn." He offered the cup. "Careful, it's hot. That saddle horn has a lot of uses. It's there for whatever goddamn need a man's got." Henry took that in, tasted the coffee. He gave the cup back. John changed the subject. "By rights, I'd wait here till Bull Hogan shows up, but it sticks in my craw, that's all, the way I been treated. The law's one thing, but Van Horn taking personal charge of the whole county, that's something else. Then there's the way the whole town acted, the other night. Last night, was it? God, seems like ages ago. Well, if it hadn't been for you—Lord knows, I'd be a ragged wreck by now. Red, he stuck by me. Your dad's not gifted with the gab, he's like me that way, but he didn't go with the crowd. So, that's about all I've got to say."

"You plan on staying out here?"

"Till there's no more fun in it." He laughed. "How about you, Henry. What's your plan?"

"I better go back to town."

"That's best." John stood up and began stamping on the fire. "You want to take this chair to the house? It's not locked. Then we'll hightail out of here."

They rode side by side, one horse in each track of an overgrown truck path. It was a peaceful time. Henry asked John why he had ridden far south toward Tunbridge Wells and then doubled back. Was it a trick?

"It was. There's only one road down around Tunbridge Wells. I figured they'd have to get horses to go in there and pick up our tracks. I'm hoping we gained an hour or two. That means Bull Hogan. He's the tracker, has a reputation for it."

"He looks stubborn," Henry said.

"You're right. Bull is a tenacious man. Quite a character. Moved into Goshen a few years back—wife and two, three kids. Before that, he spent time in one of those BLM horse-taming programs. You know, where model prisoners work with wild horses?"

"Bull was a con?"

"Pretty, isn't it? Ex-con turns deputy sheriff. What I hear is, Pierre Labray was having trouble with this pricey filly he'd bought. Lovely animal, but she wouldn't learn to take the bit. Oh, Pierre could get her bridled all right, but it was always somewhat of a hassle—irritating. Well, somebody told him there was this guy had the touch. Like gypsies have? Some cowpokes, too, some women. Winona Turpin's one. A run-of-the-mill person, like me, for instance—we manage, but we're missing that little whatever it is. Well, Bull's got it. Pierre contacted him. They hit it off from the first, that's what I was told."

"Is he dangerous?"

"Bull? Damned if I know. I guess any man is dangerous, if the situation is right."

"Yeah."

Heavy grey clouds began piling up in the west and when the two riders topped a rise and looked down on the Sagehen River they met a cool wind. John said, "Looks like we're in for a quick switch. Might even be snow."

Chapter 17

THEY CAUGHT UP with Henry near the place where a two-track road crosses a meadow to the old ford that is still used by riders in a hurry. It cuts at least a mile and a half from a valley crossing.

Two riders. Henry watched them come from the east, at a gallop, on Fox Road. One man was big, he rode a tall sorrel. The other man was thin and his horse looked just like Dan. Henry remembered what brother Brent had said: "The whole Sagehen isn't big enough for the two of us." That had been only a few weeks before the fight, when Brent received one too many orders and shouted terrible things, and Dad shouted back and they went to wrestling and punching and gasping, and Henry had been a part of that fight, at the edge of it, screaming scared. Afterwards, Henry kept on looking up to Brent, but nothing stayed quite the same.

He stood in the stirrups to ease the raw saddle rash on his inner thighs where his thin green corduroys hadn't been protection enough. Red rode up and reined in. Dan snorted; he was breathing hard. Red asked, "You about finished, Henry? You through fooling around?"

Henry nodded.

Bull Hogan was holding the sorrel a few paces back, but within ear-shot. He said, "Henry, there's no witnesses to you opening that cell door, but we all know you did it. There's no warrant out, yet. I've got no orders to arrest you, yet. Now then, we are in a hurry and I am asking you where John Moss went."

Henry gripped the saddle horn. It has many uses, he remembered. His teeth were clamped together, they made his jaw ache.

Red tried. "Henry, what the man is getting at is, you could show some cooperation here. It could make a difference, later, for you."

Henry looked away, shifted in the saddle, but his mouth was as shut as ever. Red knew better than to push any further. His son had been in a clam act for months. Nothing seemed to reach him. Belle had issued a warning: "No fighting, Red. If fighting happens, I am out of here. You know I mean it. Patience. We can learn patience." But Red's fuse had burned dangerously low. "What about Jug here?" he asked.

"He's mine."

"Oh he is, is he? Since when?"

"John's leaving the Sagehen, wanted Jug to be in good hands."

Plain old, garden-variety jealousy swept Red, made him speechless. That counted as a few moments of patience. He dismounted and fussed with Dan's cinch.

Bull said, "Henry, you listen to me. The sheriff had to deputize your dad; no way we could get him to stay back; that's on account of you mixing into this thing. Red's here to keep me in line." He waited. "You know what I'm saying?"

Henry knew, and it was a new twist, something he would never have guessed. He faced Bull, directly, for the first time. "Now we are getting someplace," Bull thought.

But Henry looked away, set his sights on the long vista, north, into the Sagehen Valley. He mumbled, "What should I do, Dad?"

Red had his head down, making a project out of Dan's cinch. He said, "It's your call, Henry. John Moss is my friend. I feel as bad as you do." Neither he nor Henry knew whether Bull Hogan heard any of that. Neither cared. Henry turned back to Bull and shook his head.

Bull didn't curse his luck, that wasn't his way. He simply shrugged and led off, gambling on the Spring Gulch Ford, and sure enough, partway across the meadow he found fresh horse tracks.

The water was low and quiet, this time of year. From a few bends downstream came faint sounds of the first of three closely-spaced rapids. The sorrel splashed across. Henry said, "Dad, did you call Mom?"

"Called her from Blackrock, then I had to go clear back to John's place and load Dan in a trailer. Trucked him and Bull's horse damned near to Tunbridge Wells."

They crossed the river and came out on a black-mud cattle trail that was strewn with fallen, yellow willow leaves. The trail wound through the willows into another meadow. Bull no longer looked for tracks, he wanted to cover ground. Hayfields, willow patches, barb-wire gates, sage flats, ditches and swales—all merged in a dream, for Henry—dog tired and his role played out.

They reached Highway 11. Bull rode north along the shoulder, leaning his bulk down from the saddle as best he could, studying the ground. He turned and rode south, then he came back, wearing a wide smile. "John's crossed the road. That narrows things down pretty well." Henry wondered what it was like, to enjoy your work, to have a reputation, to be in charge of something.

They rested the horses on the west side of the highway. A few cars passed. A state patrol cruiser came from the south, glided to a stop. The trooper rolled down his window. Henry recognized him, Bert Chalmers, ex-cowboy. Highway 11 was a part of his regular beat. He stuck his head out. "Just had a piece of luck. A driver saw Brownie, on the Lizard. Maybe twenty minutes ago."

Of all the Jedediahs' southern ridges, only one has a name, the Lizard. It's the highest and it thrusts farther into the valley. The highway makes a long loop to round it. The Lizard is rocky and cliff-lined, but topped with old-growth Douglas fir.

Bull said, "John Moss has made his first mistake. Did you radio Pierre?"

"Yup. "

Henry dismounted and hung onto the stirrup leathers, watched the three men trade ideas. Red wasn't saying much. Another cruiser arrived. Pierre Labray. Bull brought him up to date. Bull's theory was that the fugitive had intended to run north to Wild Horse Canyon, where a sketchy but usable trail crossed the range. "He ran out of time," Bull concluded. "He took to the Lizard. He'll run into rimrock, no way through, not with a horse, and John Moss is not about to leave that horse behind."

The sheriff said, "Here's what we'll do: Bert, you and I patrol the roads, especially south of here. Bull, you get up on that next ridge, cover the north side of the Lizard. Red, take the Lizard, south side. Now listen, this isn't a life-and-death matter, so don't go making it into one. Catch him up, talk him down, that's all. Actually, I'm a little surprised at John Moss running off, making such a big deal out of this."

Bull chuckled. "John Moss is a bit of a joker, Pierre. That's what I'm told."

Red was shaking his head. He tugged Dan forward, offered the reins to Bert Chalmers and spoke to Labray. "Sorry, Sheriff, I appreciate you letting me in on this—I can't go on with it—can't imagine me coming up to my friend and arresting him."

"Now, Red, you can't just go doing something like that."

"I signed on because of my son—well, hell, John Moss's broken no law worth diddly-shit."

"You'll get up there on the Lizard, if I tell you to." Labray was facing Red in a hard way, a little hot around the neck.

Bert Chalmers said, "Pierre, I wouldn't mind a spell in the saddle."

Labray stepped back and threw up his hands. "Why do I bother? My God, all this fuss and feathers for something don't amount to..." He stopped, on the edge of saying "diddly-shit."

Chalmers started adjusting Dan's stirrups. He said, "Weather report is cold and wind, maybe snow."

Bull nodded. "Thought so. Well, I'm not about to freeze my ass off all night up there on the ridge. This is mainly Van Horn's show and I'm gettin' weary of it."

Labray snapped at him. "You got that wrong, Bull. This is my show and I'll be the one who sends up a flare for when you come back down."

Bull gave a pull at his hat, signifying "OK, you're the boss," and to hide his expression. He was suspecting that the saddle burr irritating Pierre Labray came from knowing that if Van Horn had been an ordinary working stiff, Labray would have told him to go fly a kite.

Chapter 18

....

 FROM A DOUGLAS FIR shelter John had watched the tableau at the highway—men, horses, patrol cars. He had seen Red Izard stand back while another man mounted Dan. Tough act for Red, a man who hated to stand still. An hour had passed. Dan's hooves were going clunk-a-tunk on shale, gaining. The sheriff's strategy was working, perfectly.

Brownie was nothing but a nuisance here; a huge beast stranded on terrain made for animals like the mule deer that suddenly materialized on the south slope of the Lizard. She posed in front of junipers, her big ears motionless, then flicking, then motionless. She tensed and went off in three high bounds, disappeared. John thought about deer. Unpredictable critters, subject to panic; also capable of stepping silently from one shelter to another, or of sticking tight, in cover, to let hunters pass by. You never knew, for sure, what a deer might choose to do.

Bull Hogan switchbacked his way, leading the sorrel. He and the sorrel were both somewhat short-winded, but Bull set a reasonable pace and he used a rest-step, which jibed nicely with his usual procedure: go, stop, stare, go. Within an hour, and only a short while before full dark, he came to a likely spot. He tied the horse and hunkered down against a fallen whitebark pine and reached for the binoculars. To his naked eye the Jedediahs above timberline looked like tilted greenswards bordered by decorative gravel. He knew better. The 8 x 40 field-of-view revealed long, layered cliffs and talus break-a-legs and dense hedges of wind-shaped brush.

It wasn't long before he spotted an animal. Deer? No. John Moss leading Brownie down the Lizard's north side, into the first grove of pines. Bull scrutinized the pines without let-up until night began to blur all distinctions. He was certain that John and the horse were sitting tight, resting up and standing pat, snug as bugs in a rug. He caught another movement, on top of the Lizard. Bert Chalmers. Bull stood and shouted and waved his arms and pointed. Bert answered in kind. They kept it up until each knew the other wasn't getting the message. Bert disappeared. The wind was beginning to howl. Where was Pierre's flare? And damned if that wasn't a high, lacy curtain of snow sailing gently along the Lizard's crest.

Rocks and down timber lay in wait, in blizzard dark, under fresh drifts. John led, Brownie stumbled behind, his breath fuming and building icicles on his muzzle. Patience. A time to match sluggish judgments with slow movement. A time of cold trance—John is with Sarah in the heat of summer. The job is new, the marriage is new. Wild Horse Canyon and a rockbound creek, Sarah stepping into its shell of cold air. She stops and John jumps to her and puts his hands on her waist, for balance. A water ouzel flips out of the spray and the roar to teeter on a wet rock, grey body on the rock's deeper grey. The ouzel disappears into rampaging water, a disappearance hard to believe. It shows again, downstream. They watch it vanish. Away from the creek, sunny meadows, late summer flowers, sharp resin smells. They scramble toward timberline.

Near the foot of the Lizard the wind was as bad as ever, but Brownie began to find decent horse footing. John cleared snow from the saddle and mounted and steered Brownie to the highway. Once across, he gave Brownie his head and closed his eyes. Sarah. In the ordinary course of events their paths wouldn't have met. She taught English and directed class plays in a country school. She was active in community affairs and in politics of the grassroots kind and was on the verge of marriage to an environmental law consultant. He and she were going to do exciting, socially relevant things. But that summer the Medicine Bow Mountains hosted giant forest fires and it wasn't long before a nearby range did the same. Sarah's town grew and boomed, furiously alive. Smoke hung low, the mountains rarely seen, Main Street full of vehicles, night and day. Bars open into morning hours. Fire fighters from Montana and from the coast mingled with chopper pilots and army transport crews, truckers and laborers, tourists in cowboy hats and ranchers in tourist garb. The town's residents joined in with a will. Everybody had been on a high for more than a week when John Moss brought a string of pack horses to a trucking point north of town. His boss had hired out his pack outfit and hunting guides for high-paying fire duty. As soon as John had the animals taken care of he treated himself to a cold bath, borrowed a clean shirt and Levis and went to town. He took his time, drifting the street, wanting a long evening, not a quick trip to oblivion. Along toward one in the morning he found himself helping a woman hoist a drunk through the crowd and into the back of a car.

She asked, "Do you mind going with me—just a few blocks? There's a steep stairway."

After they dumped the drunk on the bed Sarah slammed the door on him. "This is the end and I'm glad." She led John into the kitchen. "I'm glad, because I guess there was always some niggling little doubt in my mind."

"There always is," John said.

"Yes, but my God, tonight he makes a play for my best friend, right in front of me. Drunk, of course—but, you know—and I wasn't just being oversensitive—hell, my friend had to run—literally run—into the street."

She began to make coffee. "This is a crazy time. And don't think I'm making a play for you."

"Yes, Ma'am."

She faced him, her hair swinging across her face. "Wipe the grin off."

He refused.

She said, "You're some other type of bastard aren't you."

His grin faded and he watched the coffee water. They both watched it. They stood there, talking for an hour or so. They never sat down. She told him she'd grown up on a Wyoming ranch. He claimed that he'd guessed that to be the case. She challenged him: how had he known? He bluffed, told some lies. She saw through them, laughed. "What a load of bullshit. You're kind of a joker, aren't you." It wasn't a question.

Later, she said, "You'd better leave." The way of it, her quick sidelong glance, was the most seductive act he'd seen in a long time. The next night they made love with sure abandon. Was it the forest fire hullabaloo, raging so closely and out of control, enveloping everybody in a collective frenzy? John never saw it that way, never even raised the question in his mind.

But Sarah did, once, at the tail end of one of their most grinding altercations. She asked, "Maybe it was all a simple mistake, because of the forest fire."

"No," he answered. As so often, she waited for more and it didn't come.

Brownie stopped. Snow hissed on a black surface of water. Sagehen River. John came awake with a jerk. He sat quietly, stupefied by cold, then he urged Brownie into the water. On the other side, Brownie stopped, shook himself, went on through willows into blank whirls of snow. John couldn't find a landmark anywhere, he gave up, left everything to the horse.

Brownie made a bad stumble. He recovered, but John lurched out of the saddle and hit a drifted-over sage. He rolled and saw stars, real ones, in immense space, out of reach in a momentary gap in the blizzard. Brownie's reins flapped past, whispering like mad black snakes. A Stetson bounced away, like a scared animal. John chased it, grinning with the pain of cold. A happy craziness took him. He saw Truth: the world is—all things have a place. He fell into a gully. Fine snow powder slanted across his face, gently, it seemed, from out of the roaring mainstream overhead. John saw the truth: if he didn't find Brownie and the bedroll, he was a goner.

Brownie was there, hipshot, snow-splattered, enduring. His eyes were nearly shut, his lashes bearing snow. John unfastened the picket rope, hooked one end to Brownie's bridle, snagged the other end around a few gnarls of sage. He unsaddled, dumped saddle and blanket and bedroll into the gully. He undid the bedroll and took off his boots and stuffed them under the saddle. One more chore—lie down, curl up, shiver to sleep.

Chapter 19

THE SNOW MELTED in less than twenty hours, except for patches in high country. Ruth Zalent went to town and waited in a line-up at the front counter at Rexall Drugs. Most people were patient, knowing that the replacement for Flora Kimball was struggling to get the hang of a check-out system new to her. Ruth made a trivial purchase and went to the back of the store and hung around, pretending an interest in the vitamin shelves. When Jerry was free she went to him. "We should talk."

He wouldn't look at her. She hated that. She waited him out. He said, "I have to be here until five, to close up."

"Six, then. I'm shopping in Goshen this afternoon. I will drop in at Nineteen Twelve."

Jerry opened the heavy glass door of Nineteen Twelve. Noisy customers occupied nine of the tables. Ruth Zalent held the tenth, in the far right corner. Jerry sidestepped toward her between closely spaced chairs and tables. She called across the hubbub, "My favorite pharmacist, what a pleasant surprise."

He sat down, miserably sober. "This is awful," she thought. "God, what a lump." She'd been served coffee and vanilla ice cream. She said, "The ice cream is excellent, as always."

A waiter came up, a youth in the regulation white shirt and black vest.

"You know," Jerry said to him, "I believe I'll have a cherry soda."

The waiter went away, Jerry watched him. Ruth tapped on the table top. "Jerry, we have to trust each other. I recognized your voice on the phone, after I had time to think back on it, and I remembered our few words about Wild Horse."

He nodded. "I'm sorry, I shouldn't have…"

"Nonsense. Please, don't talk that way. We're in this together. All right? You agree? And, I want to report." She leaned close. "Your turn, Jerry. Say something."

He pulled a napkin from a paper bouquet that splayed up from a tall, green glass. "Ms. Zalent, people come in through the back door at the drug store, they go into the office. Sometimes the voices are loud. Happy loud voices. Large sums are involved. Very big. Money…"

He paused and she urged. "Money, yes, of course. Makes the world go round."

"Therefore—what, uh, came to your mailbox—I'm hoping that's not very much, really. That's what I tell myself."

"Yes, I'll second that. And it's all blood money, anyway. That's the way I look at it. Just paper, passing through."

"Passing through," he repeated. The waiter brought his soda. He poked into it with the long silver spoon.

Ruth said, "All right, now to business. The easement on the Barrows property cost us eighty-five thousand. The lawyer got five. Jerry, did you ever stop to think how an ordinary law-abiding woman opens a checking account with a bag full of greenbacks? Never mind, I managed it. Found me a lawyer young, bold and hungry. Once landed, the lawyer did a bang-up job. But now I hear this awful rumor, to the effect that Far Haven will get their hotel in spite of our easement."

"Yes, maybe, by offsetting it a little, onto the Barrows grazing lease." Now that they were on the safer ground of public affairs, he spoke a little more freely. He told her what he knew, which was quite a lot. A land swap was in the works, Far Haven to receive full title to part of the Barrows grazing allotment and the federal government to receive, in exchange, a quarter section of private land located at the north border of the Jedediah National Forest.

Ruth asked if the quarter section was worth anything, in terms of environmental quality or economic potential. "Not as far as anybody knows," he answered. "It's overgrazed sheep country. Foothills and desert and a seep. Far Haven promises to fix the seep, fence it against livestock, put in amenities."

"Amenities."

"Outhouse, picnic tables, drinking water spigot."

"Is that all? And who on earth would actually use those?"

"Hunters, I guess, maybe a few bikers. The Jedediah forest supervisor indicates he's inclined to look favorably on the offer. The Instar Corporation holds an option on the section. An absentee owner is willing to get his investment back. Instar will buy from him, sell to Far Haven. Then the land swap can happen."

"So intricate. So clever. How did you learn all this?"

"Like I said, people in the office. Smoke Creek is the broker."

"The outfit with a finger on every lever."

"Yes. They've already negotiated federal leases for ski runs and tramway and all that."

"I know."

He was digging deeply, vigorously into the hard, old-style ice cream, levering it into chunks. Some of the softer stuff overflowed, ran down the glass to the table. Jerry didn't notice. Ruth felt better, thinking, "Now that he's started, maybe I'll have trouble shutting him up."

He said, "The new idea is interfacing human spaces and natural spaces—in creative ways—a lot of talk about that. They call it a 'greenway.' It's the way development will go, in the twenty-first century. What happens in the Sagehen will be a model—a breakthrough."

She suspected him of a buried sense of irony. She said, "Interfacing, I hate that, so very much."

He looked at her, directly and for longer than half a moment. "Yes," he said, and their conspiracy seemed sealed, and Ruth was emboldened to ask, "Jerry, why do you stand and watch the mountains?"

"Oh, it's just a habit I got into. It doesn't work any more."

Ruth looked across the crowd to the long, marble-slabbed fountain where waitpersons worked like demons. "Didn't you ever wonder why I took an interest in Wild Horse?"

"I assumed you were an environmentalist."

She laughed. "I don't belong to anything. I don't even subscribe to save-the-earth slicks. I'm a lot more selfish, want those mountains for myself."

"I'm selfish too," he said.

The admissions silenced them; for a while they gave in to the rackety kaleidoscope of Nineteen Twelve, the enclave where people gathered to be animated with each other, to be away from the drab rigor outside—courthouse, boarded-up storefronts. Goshen, the unpromising land. Jerry finished his soda.

Ruth said, "I take frequent walks, on my five acres and into the foothills. Much of the time I daydream. Once, I saw long-ago people. They weren't digging the ground for roots or building shelters, all that archaeological jazz. They were standing around, talking. I can't remember their faces, but I can still call up the sounds of their voices. Of course, I made it all up, but it was very real. And the desert I was standing on and the mountains in the far background of my dreaming—what were they? I have to ask myself: Do I ever see the land the way it really is?"

Jerry was watching the action across the room. He held his soda glass in a tight grip.

Ruth said, "There are other times when I'm less fanciful. One day I put a bobcat on top of actually existing cliffs, above town."

"I'm sure bobcats have been up there, some time in the past."

She laughed. "I'm sure they have. Maybe even now, at night, while we're all asleep." She wondered how he spent his nights.

He said, "Those cliffs have senior class years painted on them."

"I noticed. Looks to me like they ran out of cliff space, somewhere in the late fifties."

"No. That's when the county built the consolidated school in Goshen." Then, surprising her, he returned to their original agenda. "Far Haven has one more problem at Wild Horse. For the government to cancel the grazing lease, there has to be good cause."

"Good cause. Well, what's their problem? Barrows gave it up, didn't he?"

"Yes, but it's been transferred to a sheep outfit, one of the big ones, up toward Monax. Gino Donnadio."

"I know him! Gino and Bea, they're practically neighbors, six or seven miles up the road from me. Are you saying there's still hope?"

"No. JT Timberlake called a meeting, at the OX. Abe Fox's ranch. You know JT?"

"By reputation. Let me guess: JT is a politician, he needs both Smoke Creek and its influence as well as the cattlemen—a winning coalition. So, bring them together, gang up on the sheep man."

He nodded, admiring her quickness, and told her the rest of it: When the cowmen saw to it that sheep wouldn't be allowed in the Sagehen, the federal land managers would have their "cause" and the Barrows lease could be canceled, with no fuss, no challenges. "Simple," he concluded, "And there's a senator in Washington to back it up."

"A senator? It's that cut and dried?"

He smiled broadly and stepped out of character for a fleeting moment. "Ms. Zalent...."

She laughed. "Wait—I know what you're about to say—and call me Ruth. Please?" Then the import of the meeting at the OX got to her. "It's hopeless. We've lost Wild Horse."

He shrugged, meaning that it had always been hopeless. "The man to see is Evan Hughes."

"Who's he?"

"Range Con, BLM."

"Who sees him? You? Me?"

"You would do a lot better job Ruth."

"All right. Tell me about Evan Hughes."

Chapter 20

··

 BROWNIE CAME OUT of the Heeaws in magnificent condition, ready for winter. In the past two days he had found nutritious grazing and the travel pace had been leisurely—seemingly aimless, as though his rider had no definite destination. But now, the Heeaws a half day's travel behind him, Brownie was stepping right along, due north. Great swells of land nearly hid the Jedediahs; their top ridges were a low jagged line at the west edge of the sage sea; evening sunlight broke between cloud strata, picked out distant mesas. An intermittent wind floated faint cries of sheep.

Brownie crested a long and gentle slope, into suddenly loud sheep noise. A small bunch of ewes ran from him, slanting downhill into sunlight to join a fringe of the main band that was flung over the sage like a big unraveling blanket. Directly opposite, a canvas-covered wagon perched near aspens and a squiggly little patch of seep-green.

From a distant wrinkle in the land came a dog—black with white markings—followed by a rider on a black horse. The rider rode with one shoulder slightly lower than the other. He wore a T-cap, grey and blue stripes, large bill. John Moss lifted a hand and put Brownie into a casual lope to a meeting place where sunlight and shadow met.

The man on the black flashed a large smile. "I'm Bryan Lashley, herder for Gino Donnadio."

"John Moss."

"We heard about you." He pointed to the dog, who had stopped and was looking back at them. "That's Jack, he does most of the work around here. Well, let's get on up to camp, you'll stay the night."

The horses ambled side by side. John said, "What was it you heard about me?"

"You're wanted for jail break and giving the sheriff a good run."

"Does that bother you any?"

"The story is you got in bad with Smoke Creek. Doesn't bother me at all."

"Didn't have much to do with Smoke Creek."

"I see. Well, I'll want to hear about it. By the way, we're headed for the Sagehen. How about you?"

"I just come from there."

"I see." He laughed. "We've got a lot to talk about." It was Bryan Lashley who did the talking. By the time they reined in at a temporary corral made of aspen poles, John knew something about coal mining at Rock Springs and the mine accident that had smashed Lashley's shoulder. And the death of his wife, in childbirth. And the baby boy who had been taken in by a sister-in-law in Kemmerer while Lashley went to drifting west, picking up temporary jobs.

"I owe Gino Donnadio," he said. "He took me in. I drove a truck in his haying crew. Donnadio took an interest in me. I don't know, some whisper from the Lord. It was this shoulder of mine. Donnadio's somewhat of a crip, himself. Next thing I knew he had me at the corrals, with Manny trying to teach me to stay on a horse." He tipped his head toward the wagon where a man sat on his heels at a cooking fire, looking at them from under a black hat. "That's Manny Gabriel, Gino's chief honcho. He's just now arrived here, to help me make the drive. Mexican. Born in *New Mexico*. He's no wetback."

John nodded, but that wasn't good enough. Lashley gave him a steady stare. "Manny's OK. He's as American as you or me."

"I hear you."

They unsaddled and stowed gear in a brown wall tent that was tucked away in the aspen grove. Lashley lifted the cover from a metal drum. "Oats here, help yourself." He led the black to the corral and turned him in with a handsome dun. John gave Brownie a handful of oats. Lashley waited, so that they would walk together to the fire.

"Manny, this is John Moss, from the Sagehen."

Manny gave a friendly enough nod and said, "I put on extra beans."

They sat up late around the fire, cool night air at their backs. At intervals the aspen fuel fluffed into a flare and died down again. Manny fed the fire and Lashley gave John the news from Monax and the Instar gold mine and the plans for another mine. John sat on a log and enjoyed the company. His throat was stiff, unused; he had hardly spoken, other than an occasional word to Brownie, since the day after the blizzard when he'd dropped in on the Hagerstroms. They'd given him bacon and bread and coffee and wished him well.

Lashley was talking about the disadvantages of learning horsemanship late in life. He ended that and said, "John, I imagine you got put in the saddle about the time you learned to walk."

"No, I was a townie, got my start on calves. My home town's a feedlot place. When the wind is in the east you know it. Down at the stockyards, we had all anybody would ever want in the way of corrals and chutes. Ranchers and cowhands had the habit of stopping in there, in the evenings.

They'd bring six-packs and spend an hour or so. Sometimes they'd bring their ropin' horses for some serious practice. There was always livestock to work: feeder calves and yearlings, cows, steers, wild horses, stallions. The cowpokes, they'd go to ropin' anything that moved: stray cats, dogs. Us kids hung around there a lot."

Lashley began to speak, but Manny pushed a hand at him. "The man hasn't got to his point yet."

"Well," said John, "what happened to us kids, down there, that's all. Some happy cowpoke'd get hold of a calf and lift a kid up on top and whoop and holler and let that calf go. Whoof! If you didn't get bucked off the first jump you'd feel like you were all set for the gold buckle at Madison Square Garden." He cleared his throat. "I'm rusty," he said. Manny smiled.

John bedded down in the wall tent, between the drum of oats and the saddle gear. Close above the canvas, aspen twigs twittered in a light wind. That was soothing, familiar. He stayed awake for a long time.

Remembering Winona, in a grey sweater and purple-grey gabardines, at one end of the Bear Bar's red vinyl couch—the OX ranch foreman at the other end and young Hendricks, mail carrier for Rural Route 2, in the middle. Winona was pointing to an antelope head that faced a bull buffalo. Those two had been staring at each other night and day since before anybody could remember. Winona had noticed a slight tipping of the antelope's head and a new look in its glass eyes. "Those two have got something going..." John, at the bar, didn't hear all of it. Winona broke into a high squeal, her eyes tearful, joyous. She happened to be looking directly at John. That was the time. It began then.

Remembering Sarah, in a pink shirt and blue denim skirt, on the street, ages ago, the time of the rampaging forest fires. She and John on the board sidewalk, only slightly drunk, Sarah telling a story about a local bigwig, and imitating him—turmoil on the sidewalk and in the street—Sarah's laughter, both of them reeling, falling against each other. "I never reminded her," he thought. "But hell, how would a person go about it?"

Sarah had written, once, since February, saying she treasured the rubber rattlesnake. John puzzled over that. Was the snake reminding her of something good or something terrible? That word, "treasure," he'd worried it to death. Finally, he wrote on a postcard, "Miss you." A few days later he mailed it. Her letter had made no mention of a lawyer or divorce papers. The postmark was Denver, July 16. No word since.

Jack sat, solemn and calm, at some distance from camp. His charges gathered slowly in long gangly bunches, moving in diagonals across dark grey slopes. The sun was about to rise.

John joined Manny at the cooking fire. Manny laid out fried bacon across a sheet of the *Monax Telegram*. A mess of eggs popped in deep bacon fat. Lashley came up from the seep, his face and hair wet. Manny dished up the eggs. He nodded to a tin box. "There's bread in there." They ate in silence. John washed dishes. By the time he'd finished with the greasy skillet Manny had struck the wall tent and was at the corral saddling the dun. Lashley rummaged in the wagon. He came out with two sets of saddle bags and put them on an aspen log to keep them from the dew. He looked around the camp. "Well, we'll be pulling out."

John asked, "How fast do these sheep travel?"

"Tonight we'll be at Quin Crossing on Chiseler Creek. Gino'll have a truck there. The truck'll come here for the wagon and tent. Then we figure two days, two and a half, from Quin Crossing to the Barrows' range. What do you think?"

"Sounds about right. I don't know sheep. Have you thought of cutting straight east from Quin Crossing, go over the Heeaws, then south?"

"No. BLM laid out the route: west side of the Heeaws, all the way."

"You'd find easy traveling on the east. Rolling desert country, like what you have here."

"How about fences?"

"Not many. Corporation ranches, over there. Each one big as half a county."

"We don't have BLM permission for that."

John shrugged and Lashley grinned. "How would we get back into the Sagehen?"

"Take Lincoln Creek. You go through an easy pass, brings you out at the DuckWing." He picked up a twig and drew a map in the dirt. "The DuckWing's not operating any longer. Smoke Creek bought it out, last spring. There's a caretaker there."

"Hardly any cowmen along the way," said Lashley. "I like the idea of that." He went to the corral. John watched him and Manny confer. They leaned back against the rails, their faces serious in the glow of sunrise. Manny laughed, quietly, looked over at John. Lashley came back. "Say, how about you coming with us, show us that route?"

"Manny's idea, or yours?"

"I was thinking it, he's the one said it."

"Well, Bryan, I don't know. Thanks for the invite. Seems sort of silly. I was putting the Sagehen behind me."

A shaggy grey cat stepped out from under the wagon. Lashley scooped her up. "John, you want to give me a hand here?"

"What's wrong with it?"

"Her hair's a mess. If you can keep a strong hold on her, I'll get my scissors."

The cat was big, and nervous, but John held two legs firmly in each hand while Lashley worked on her with his fingers, picking apart burred hair mats, cutting away the worst of them. John remarked that a long-hair would do better indoors.

"I know," Lashley said. "Gino insists every sheep camp's got to have its cat. I drew this one. So, you decided yet? Three days, at most. You're not in any real trouble down in the Sagehen, are you?"

John gave him a look. "I'll be the judge of that."

"Didn't mean to speak out of turn." But Bryan Lashley was a hard man to put down. He grinned. "Got the nerve to turn sheeper for a while?"

"That what Manny was laughing at?"

"No, no. I was telling him what a great show him and me are going to make, down there in cattle country—a crippled sheeper and a mean-looking Mex. Funny, eh?"

"Be even funnier with a jailbird tagging along." They laughed and John looked over at Manny and nodded.

Chapter 21

EVAN HUGHES FACED Ruth Zalent. He had been giving her a runaround and felt ashamed, but she leaned across his desk and wasn't about to quit.

"Answer a simple question," she said. "Does Gino Donnadio have a valid grazing lease in the Sagehen, or does he not?"

"There's a document," Evan said, "I can show you." He swiveled and pulled open a file drawer.

"Mr. Hughes, please, let us not descend to documents. I'll ask you this: Are you perfectly satisfied with the answers you have been handing me?"

"Not perfectly, but that doesn't mean I am at liberty to speak for other people, or get my personal opinions mixed into this."

"Yes, yes—we've been all over that, and I accept that your opposite number at Jedediah National Forest has direct supervision over Donnadio's lease—and so on. Wait, I'll try something different. Let me give you my own view of the situation."

"Please do."

"Possession is nine tenths of the law. I want to see those sheep possess that grazing, and hold it, against Far Haven."

Evan pulled in his bureaucrat horns and felt better. "That's interesting. What you just said is my exact same reasoning."

"Now we're getting someplace," Ruth said.

He raised a hand. "Unfortunately, there have been developments, stemming from that meeting at the OX. One, the ranchers are all set to ride north, with rifles. Two, a directive from..."

"Uh oh," she cut in. "Let me guess. A sudden communication from Washington. Do I get a cigar?"

Evan was surprised and showed it. "Ms. Zalent, you appear to be unusually perceptive—on all of this. Are you with some organization?"

She laughed. "No, only a card carrying member of the general public, although I do read printed material, like a house afire. I am disgustingly well informed. So then, the position is, somebody's senator made a phone call. There's your sudden new development."

Evan tugged at his ear.

"Stop me if I'm wrong," she continued. "The word from on high went on some fast track that I couldn't possibly know about, and filtered down to the desk of your colleague—what's his name?"

"Dave Darwin. Go on."

"Cleared of gobbledygook, the message David Darwin received was to this effect: Expedite the land swap.

Evan shifted his attention to the bookcase across the room, to the Zuni vase, to the picture on the wall—a winter scene, Montana mountains. "You don't need me to tell you anything," he said.

"He looks so sad, so beaten," she thought. "Do I coddle him or berate him? Don't be silly, Ruth. Be kind. No, that would be the worst thing you could do."

He solved her dilemma by shedding what was left of his discreet BLM role. "Gino Donnadio called me this morning, said his herder had the band on the move. They'll be at Quin Crossing by tonight."

She raised her brows, questioning, in suspense.

"I told him to come ahead."

She blurted, "Then you haven't quite given up."

Again, he was examining the picture on the wall. "Technically my— technically I'm still covered. Dave is delaying his environmental evaluation as long as possible. He can hold out for another couple of days, that's all. Now you know everything."

"Well, hardly everything, but thank you, for speaking plainly." Her mind raced, trying to penetrate what tomorrow held—and the day after that. She pictured Donnadio's sheep flowing across sage slopes, like oatmeal porridge, pouring into the Sagehen, down the full length of the valley—then she saw men with guns. She looked at the man on the other side of the desk. She and he read each other, perfectly. He even nodded, slightly. "The sheep cross into the Sagehen tomorrow. What right do I have… to send others into danger? I think I'll have to call it off. There's still time."

She put the Wild Horse campaign into perspective: Jerry Haun's daring theft, her own equally gutsy laundering of money and her work with the Monax lawyer, her clever maneuvering here, in this office. And this man, Hughes, wanting so badly to play the sheep card, the last one in their hand. And all these plans, so interesting and laced with a seasoning of hope—all turned to dust, canceled by guns. She trembled with anger.

Evan wasn't looking at her. He picked up a pencil and broke it and threw it into the plastic wastepaper basket where it made a timid rustling sound.

Jerry Haun had been wrong. The man to see was not Evan Hughes. There was no real man to see. "Seeing men" was to play their game. Ruth's bitter resignation was complete. She stood and went to the doorway. Out of her despair came a perverse desire, to keep Evan Hughes away from the phone. Maybe a few minutes could make a difference. Maybe the evolving scheme of things would reach a critical moment wherein Gino Donnadio digs in his heels, says, "Too late, BLM, we're coming through." And if fighting is always the final solution, then go to it. Ruth would take a side and cheer. It was against her training, her reasoned convictions, her world view. But she gave in to it. "One more question," she said, "and I know you're busy, but this has been bugging me for some time. What is an AUM?"

He looked up, surprised, and shrugged and told her. "It stands for Animal Units per Month. It's an estimate of the number of grazers a given acreage will support, for a month. The basic unit is a presumably typical cow and her calf. Three sheep equal one cow, and so on."

"Like, the AUM for the Barrows area would be larger than for the Shadow Mountain area?"

"Yes, most definitely. That Barrows grazing has been under-utilized for years. It has the best overall rating in all the Sagehen, actually appears to be pointed in the direction of ecological stability—whatever that means. Another hundred years, then we'll see."

"How do you estimate 'directions' and 'stability' and all that?"

"There are a zillion variables. Not like physics. In theory we analyze each plant community by species composition, soil type, slope exposure, precipitation and—especially—rare and endangered things. Not just by palatability to livestock. But we are, all of us, way behind on such work. In real life we spend most of our time making like lawyers."

"This is fascinating," she said.

He gave her a skeptical look, but couldn't resist. "I'll show you. Let's go to the herbarium."

"I'd like nothing better."

He ushered her into a room at the end of the hallway and turned on the fluorescents and went to a rank of metal cabinets. He pulled a few large folders and spread them, open, in a row on a long table. He pointed to a dried plant that was taped to an absorbent sheet of paper. It was pale and grey and fuzzy.

"Pussytoes," Ruth said.

"Bingo! There are a number of species, across the country. Low palatability. We might call this an indicator plant. It has weed traits. In our area—the Sagehen—we can define a weed as a species that flourishes in exposed, usually overgrazed, soils. A true weed is a colonizer, an opportunist, tends to take over in places where native vegetation is badly stressed. There are exceptions, of course."

Time passed. Evan, and then Ruth, became absorbed in structures of arid ranges, the growing plant stuff that contributes stability, or fragility—and character. Finally, Evan started to close the folders. He apologized. "I get carried away, talk like a...professor. This kind of thing is boring to most people."

"Not to me," she said, but now her thoughts shifted elsewhere: Run, sheep, run.

He turned out the lights. "I'll get on the phone, see how Dave's coming along."

"And Donnadio?"

"All in good time."

She said no more. She and this range con were walking some very fine lines.

He went with her to the reception area and invited her to drop in again. "Anytime."

She guessed that he meant it.

Chapter 22

 THEY PUSHED SHEEP ALL DAY, in cold rain. The band moved over the land like a huge noisy skein stinking of wet wool. Jack ranged the fringes, dogging patiently along. The fringe sheep were accustomed to him, they had long ago worked out proper working distances. Behind Jack the three horses came at a walk, their riders hunched against the wind. As darkness came on, there was a break in the cloud cover and a few stars showed for a few moments.

Manny Gabriel, riding the left flank, decided the storm would taper off during the night. He rode up on Jack and peered ahead. The slope was steepening, and there was Chiseler Creek—a scraggle of cottonwood and willow and tall sage marked its course. Manny found what he was looking for, the truck, and nearby, a ruby flickering. Good. They'd build that fire into a roar and hunker down and shake out the shivers. He put the dun into a trot, cutting through the band, sending sheep into sudden scampers.

Linc Sutton stood quietly at the hood of the truck, watching Manny ride in. He let Manny find for himself the picket line stretched between two cottonwoods, the hay bales, the supplies in the bed of the truck, neatly tarped over. Old Linc held to a certain old-fashioned etiquette that frowned on excess speech. From the truck cab came the tail end of the six o'clock news. Trouble everywhere. That suited Linc. He went to the cab door, cracked it open to catch the weather report. Manny joined him. They stood together, rain dripping from their hats. "Clearing," Linc said.

Manny murmured something and walked into the embrace of the fire's heat and light. He tossed a couple of sagebrush teasers onto the coals. They sparked and brightened. Linc brought in some dry dead willow and cottonwood and made a neat pile. He sat on his heels and roused the fire and fed it.

Manny said, "We got a cowman with us. John Moss."

"Oh?"

"We'll go down the east side of the Heeaws. This John Moss seems to know all that country. Better traveling. Tell Gino."

"All right. The rumor is, cowmen are set to block off the north end of the Sagehen."

Manny considered that. "Does Gino know?"

"Yup. He says it might be all bluff, and we're to call it. But if there's trouble, don't go bullin' through."

Linc kept quiet about what he'd overheard while tucking some last-minute groceries into the load: Bea Donnadio asking Gino if he thought it wise to send Manny into the Sagehen, and Gino's reply: "Can't be making exceptions."

Linc was glad not to be riding south with Manny. He told himself it was the hardness in the man, but Linc had to admit that a lot of that came from stubborn loyalty to Gino. Linc thought he understood the loyalty part; a man would be bound to have a special attitude toward a boss who hired a drifter and, by-and-by, brought him along to be top hand, and then set him up to ramrod the whole shebang—Anglos and Basques, Chicanos and Indians and, lately, Latinos from God knew where. They all put out the work, for Manny, no question about that. They respected him, no question about that, either—everybody reserving, of course, full bitching rights. Some swore that a smile from Manny was about as common as a bluebird in January; others said that was an exaggeration; others, Linc Sutton among them, were in no position to gripe on that score. And then, there was Marita. She had a brightness about her and a shy-friendly manner, and these qualities in Manny's wife made the headquarters ranch that much better a place to come into after a few weeks or months on the range. Marita spoke poor English, she was an unregistered "alien," but nobody who worked Donnadio's big sheep bands would have breathed a word of that, not even suspicious, grudge-bearing Linc Sutton. Prickly old bachelor, he was quick to make moral judgments. He'd made one when Bryan Lashley started working for Donnadio. Too agreeable, was Linc's verdict. Friendly to the point of brown-nosing. But time had passed. One day Linc caught Manny and Bryan standing right in front of Gino, staring into each other's faces, laughing, their mouths wide open. Linc had to conclude that, somehow or other, Bryan Lashley had won the right to stay on.

Chapter 23

 JAIMIE DELLUMS, a young cowboy, caretaking at the DuckWing, stopped raking ashes from the kitchen range, cocked his head, couldn't believe what he was hearing. He grabbed his hat and ran outside and stood amazed. The east pasture looked like it was being covered by huge flakes of dirty snow spread by a slow and relentless breeze. Jaimie ran into the house and punched out the number of Amos Snow, OX foreman.

"Amos here."

"Amos, the sheep've showed up."

"Who's this?"

"Jaimie Dellums."

"Where you at?"

"DuckWing, where'd you think?"

"I'll be damned. How many?"

"God, Amos, I don't know. Hundreds. They're piling in here from the old cattle driveway out of the Heeaws—the fence is down up there."

"Well, what about that! They've made an end run. Sit tight, Jaimie, I'll contact the boys up north."

"OK, I'll hold 'em here."

"Jaimie, I said sit tight. I didn't say anything about holdin'. Don't *do* anything. I'll be right out."

"OK, Amos." He hung up and ran outside. Some of the sheep had advanced to the barbed wire on the east side of the barnyard. Jaimie noticed a black-and-white dog moseying along the north side of the pasture, and then a rider showed, on a black horse, at a hard gallop. The rider waved. Jaimie didn't return the greeting. Instead, he trotted back into the house and rummaged in a drawer of the sideboard, picked out a clip of 30-caliber ammo, pocketed it. He took his rifle from its wall rack and put it in the back porch, behind the wood box. He stepped into the yard. The black horse slowed to a trot, then stopped. The rider's smile, so high, wide and handsome, struck Jaimie as offensive, and he wished he had his bay mare. She'd been loaned to one of his brothers who had a plum of a job guiding for an outfitter on the west side of the Jedediahs.

Lashley caught the fierce stare, up-tilted chin, flat-crowned Stetson tipped low over the forehead. He dismounted. "Sorry about this." He explained that they'd planned on pushing the sheep to Fox Road and along that to the river, but the lead ewes found a break in the pasture fence. "Well, you know sheep. Follow the leader, they're good at that."

"I don't know sheep," Jaimie said. "You can't run sheep in here. This is the Sagehen. What the fuck you think you're doing?"

"Following orders," Lashley said. "BLM and U.S. Forest Service. Let's not you and me make a big mountain out of this. I'll get these critters out of your way before dark."

The fight itch was in Jaimie, but he'd been told to wait, by no less a man than Amos Snow, Abe Fox's honcho.

Lashley turned and prepared to mount, thinking that, by a whisker, he'd squeaked through, but Jack spotted Jaimie's dog, a big, buffalo-colored animal who happened to be returning from an investigation of the south side of the pasture, where sheep were packed close against the barbed wire fence. Jack slipped under the lower wire and met the other dog for a brief hostile inspection. Jaimie called, "Dallas, get back here," but Dallas had committed himself. He and Jack jumped into a snarling stand-up. Dallas soon had Jack in a strong neckskin bite and he was not about to let go.

Lashley's first kick missed, his second struck Dallas, made him break away, but the dogs came together again and Jaimie yelled, "Fucking sheeper, get away from my dog." He came at Lashley, head down, punching. His reach was shorter, but Lashley's left shoulder and arm were stiff and slow. They went at it. A few moments later, Amos Snow and Abe Fox drove into the yard, observed two men circling each other, and two dogs rolling and snapping and snarling.

Amos sighed. "I told him to sit tight."

Abe asked, "How old is that Jaimie?"

"Eighteen, nineteen."

"You'd think he would have grown into some sense by now." Abe shifted on the pickup's high seat, reluctant to begin. He would be seventy-four in December, had come to know age as a certainty. New pains in right hip and knee seemed to have settled in for the duration.

Amos said, "I don't want to judge Jaimie ahead of time. I'll go see what's really occurred here." He opened the cab door, no more eager than Abe, to begin. At fifty-six and a widower, Amos had recently come into a fascinating relationship with the school-bus driver, one of Jaimie's aunts. He knew, therefore, the Dellums family's theories about Jaimie, the most prevalent being that his two older brothers had spoiled him rotten, which would account for his turning into a troublemaker. His mother believed none of that; she had her own ideas, but didn't spread them around; she'd done what a mother has to do, gone ahead and raised her children and stood by them. From her, the three boys learned loyalty. That's why Jaimie had parted with his mare. Terrence needed her more than he did. Jaimie knew Terrence would bring the mare back, not a day later than agreed.

Amos trotted into the yard and stepped between Jaimie and Lashley, told them to quit. He kicked the dogs apart. Jaimie's nose was dripping red. Amos handed him a handkerchief. Lashley stood quietly, kneading his shoulder. His face was smeared with blood, Jaimie's and his own. Amos looked him over, spoke in his low, neutral voice, a tone few in the Sagehen could emulate. "All right, sheep man, what's going on?"

Lashley said, "The dogs started it. There's no real problem here."

Jaimie sneered and spit. "The hell there isn't."

Amos said, "Well, we'll straighten this out."

Abe Fox, out of the cab now, yelled to Amos. "Tell that man the truth. His sheep go back north, pronto. Don't go negotiating."

Amos looked out over the field of sheep, twitched an eyebrow. "Good heavens, Abe, I wouldn't dream of it."

"Who's he?" Lashley asked.

"That's Abe Fox. What he says pretty much goes."

"I see." Lashley turned back to Jaimie who stood close, bristly, his thumbs propped against a big oval of belt silver. Lashley said, "No hard feelings, but you'll have to quit looking at me like that."

Abe joined them. "Jaimie," he said, "I'd appreciate you making a big pot of coffee. We'll be having company."

Jaimie looked for his hat, found it, jammed it on and stalked off. Amos picked up the trailing reins of the black horse. Jack had moved to the fence and was crouched there, staring at Dallas. Lashley went to him, squatted and spoke. "Easy, dog. Let's have a look." Jack winced when Lashley parted his neck fur to expose bloody skin punctures. "Not too bad, Jack. This'll heal up. Don't go making a big deal out of it. We've all got to keep cool. One step at a time. You hear me?" He sneaked a look uphill, to the brushy rise beyond the pasture. Nothing. Good, they were lying low, keeping to the agreement. There had been some awkward discussion, Manny insisting that he would be the one to ride down and straighten things out with the DuckWing caretaker. Lashley persuaded him otherwise. "I'm a talker—that's maybe all I'm really good at. Right now, that's what's needed." John had offered, saying, "I know the man down there; he's young, carries a chip on his shoulder." Manny and Lashley met that with grins, savoring images of a fugitive cowman speaking on behalf of a thousand head of invading sheep.

Lashley had summed up: "I'll go. Slow and easy. Gino wants it that way."

Manny had to agree, said, "We'll sit tight here, Bryan. Go do the talking."

Chapter 24

 LEONA HAGERSTROM RODE the school bus, homeward. Most of the students had subsided into quiet reverie, gazing blankly through the windows, watching the Sagehen go by, the lines and subtle changeful colors that they all knew so well, without ever having stopped to look. Ralph Gibbs and Susan Lansbury were still doing their bantering/flirting thing, but they too were quieter now. Leona wished that Henry Izard would quit trying to horn in on Susan and Ralph. Leona knew that Henry was still under investigation as an accomplice in John Moss's jailbreak—everybody on the school bus knew that—but it was old knowledge; Henry's day of notoriety had passed. He was now, in Leona's judgment, just another goofus trying to fit in at Goshen Central—and trying to make Susan notice him. Pathetic.

Henry did quit, for the moment. He settled back into the bus seat, feeling suddenly worn out. He looked through the dusty window, wondered if John Moss was still out there playing outlaw. He didn't wonder for long. School, Goshen, the wide world—these were the pressing challenges. His adventures with John had settled into the past; even the glamor and worry connected with the jailbreak investigation were losing ground in his consciousness—all in the space of a few days. There was a daily reminder, though: taking care of Jug. Dad had pulled a fast one. "All right, Henry, you got yourself a horse. We'll make room for him in the shed, with Dan. Which horse chores you want, morning or evening?"

The bus nosed onto the gravel lot next to Simms' Super Valu. The doors opened, the students separated quietly, townies to the street, ranch kids to three cars parked on the far side of the dumpster. Leona Hagerstrom and her brother would be the last to get home; they had to drop class-mates at two ranches before they reached their own.

Claude Deal asked Henry, "You comin' over?" Claude had a basket mounted at one end of the asphalt pad at the View Motel.

"Yeah," said Henry. "I'll be over." First, though, Henry had to draw water, fork manure and hay and straw.

Ralph Gibbs, an alert young man, stopped in his tracks, yelled, "Hey, what's wrong with this town?"

Susan Lansbury called back, "Give me an hour, I'll tell you."

"No," he said. "I mean it."

Somebody else said, "Extra dead. Yeah, you're right." Nobody laughed, they'd all sensed by now a drastic downshift in the normal quietude of their town.

Ralph said, "Cars. Vehicles. Where's all the goddamn vehicles?"

Meanwhile, a townie had slipped into Simms' to buy a candy bar. She came back on the run. "All hell's broke loose, on the DuckWing!"

"What?"

"Sheep. Hundreds of sheep."

A few town kids made a rush for ranch kids' cars and started to cram themselves in; others went looking. The bus driver, Nel Dellums, called everyone back. "Come on, come on, we'll swing over that way." When she had them all seated, she said, "Discipline, understand? We're all still on school bus time. This will be just a detour on the regular run." The doors thudded shut, the bus turned and trundled away, keeping precisely to its speed limit, down Highway 11 to Fox Road, then east.

Winona Turpin drove, recklessly, the rough track to the DuckWing. Ed Turpin was seated next to her, Flora in the back. Florence Turpin had stayed at the ranch, to continue the packing and crating of family belongings. There had been car trouble and then Ed and Florence spent a good twenty minutes arguing over whether to take the furniture with them to Phoenix, or auction it. Florence had her way. No auction.

Winona had half a wish that the old Chevy would strike its oil pan on a rock and bleed to death. She was angry and couldn't find anybody to blame. She rolled down her window, smelled the perfumes of autumn willow and cottonwood and grasses. "Dad, remember when they had the turkey shoot, over there on the DuckWing's sage flat?"

"Which one?" He turned to Flora, his smile was the one reserved for folks outside the family. "Flora, you ever been to a turkey shoot?"

Flora shook her head and sealed her decision to leave the TN. She and Ed had hit it off well and Florence had been welcoming, in a distracted way, and Flora would never forget Ed's coming so decisively to her aid on that bad day at Blackrock. But she had to face this: she'd become another wedge between father and daughter. The stubborn old man's kindness was genuine, and safe; nevertheless, Flora had to get away from it. Tomorrow, she decided. Go, with Winona, to Marya's, pack, go to Goshen. She knew the manager at Nineteen Twelve. Maybe there would be a position open, now that some of his employees had gone back to school.

Winona said, through tight lips, "I'm talking about the shoot where Ken won a turkey. I took a try too, hit the target, got inside the first circle. Not bad, for a 10-year-old."

Ed nodded. He was looking straight ahead. "Ken could've been a top-notch shooter, if he'd kept at it."

Flora wanted to grab Ed's battered Stetson and beat him over the head. Couldn't he see what he was doing?

Winona said, "Dad, why'n hell are we putting our noses into this sheep thing? We're out of everything, now."

He didn't answer. Ahead of them, a long metallic, multicolored snake sparkled in late afternoon—cars and trucks perched on both sides of the narrow road. Winona parked, they walked to the driveway. It was easy to find the focus of events; nearly everyone was facing a cattlemen's consultation at the back side of the house. Abe Fox and Shawn Lynch held seats of honor on the porch steps, Shawn in his jovial, well-fed manner, Abe stiff and gaunt, his hat tipped low and to one side against the sun. Other ranchers made a rough half-circle in front of the porch, same standing, some on their haunches. At Abe's left, leaning on a porch rail, Lars Hamil. In the doorway, scowling from under his hat, Jaimie Dellums. Off to one side, his back against the house, Bryan Lashley. And standing among ordinary folks— cowboys and townspeople—JT Timberlake.

Ed Turpin started to work his way through the crowd; people made way for him; Winona held back. Flora said, "Go on, go with your dad. I'll see you later." Winona had a stubborn stillness on her face—Flora knew it well, but Flora resisted, with a hardness of her own. "Go," she said, and gave her a push. Winona's eyes widened, not in anger, in surprise.

Flora backed away, keeping her gaze on the ground, avoiding eye contacts. She walked to the barbed wire fence. Vincent Van Horn was there too, but further along. "Smart position," Flora thought, "staying in the background. Well now, if that isn't Marya, cuddled right up to Vince and her hair down across half her face like a TV ad and she's got on the fluffy come-pet-me jacket." Flora turned the other way. A gaggle of young kids were playing with the fence, hanging on it, twanging it, picking at barbs.

The parents stood back, bemused, watching for signs of decision in the men at the porch.

Flora looked across the valley. It was a grand vista and a multicolored map. The Jeds in blues and greys, only beginning to be tinged by sunset. River bends and fields and marshes and sage benches. Clear boundaries. Summer had gone, taking away camouflage, revealing the fundamental layout. The roads were empty now, except for the sheriff's cruiser, approaching from the north, and the yellow school bus and a dark green BLM pickup that was slowing to a stop behind the Turpins' Chevy. A woman near Flora smiled and said, "Now everybody's here."

Evan Hughes tried to squeeze through the tight pack in front of the porch. One of the cowhands crossed his arms, refused to move an inch. He looked like a mean cuss, but he wasn't. Evan turned sidewise, brushed past Horace Giles, a pal of Jaimie Dellums, a hell-raiser. His rounded-eye stare was hard to take. Evan lost his balance, fell against the sturdy body of Pancho Jones and Pancho grabbed nearby shoulders, creating a wave of disturbance. Abe Fox craned his neck to see what was going on. Pancho glared at Evan, growled, "Hey there, Government Man, watch yourself." Then he winked.

Evan gained the front rank and hunkered down next to Sturling Crawford, a rancher whose land possessed a special attraction: a four-acre marsh that had been fenced against livestock for generations, because it was up-hill from the well. Evan had found several prizes there, the greatest being a showy, short-stemmed species of hawkweed, growing in deep muck. Crawford had guffawed at Evan's delight, but Evan stood up to that, brushed his hand across the hawkweed's yellow flowers, and said, "Sturling, what you have here is more precious than gold."

"It's decided then," Abe Fox said. "In the morning. Meanwhile, somebody get over on the east side, fix that break in the fence."

Evan asked, "What is it you've decided, Abe?"

"Donnadio's bunch of woolies go back where they came from, that's all."

Crawford leaned close to Evan, murmured, "We're all worked up pretty high."

"I know it, Sturling." He kept his gaze on the three leaders, the long-time Sagebrush Rebels: Abe Fox, Shawn Lynch, Lars Hamil. He detected no sign of weakness, no disunity, and the rest of the crowd seemed to be solidly with them. The fact that Ed Turpin stood off to one side, hands in pockets and looking glum, probably meant nothing other than his sense of propriety: he had lost his ranch, should no longer claim a large voice in Sagehen affairs.

Evan Hughes' opposition would be a solo act, and he knew it, and he didn't even have the backup of his own agency. For some reason, news of the crisis at the DuckWing had been late in reaching BLM headquarters, but as soon as Evan heard that Donnadio's sheep were in jeopardy he went to the side door and ran to his pickup, away from the phone, away from milk-toast orders, or cautionary advice from Dave Darwin. Now, in the thick of the action, at the center of Sagehen power, he felt as helpless as a heel-roped steer, strung out between his own lonesome, inner man who was apt to throw a tantrum and lose the whole game, and the outer man dressed in government issue. But he would give it a try, before going home to kick the refrigerator and think about resigning from BLM.

He tried to address everybody, not just those at the porch. "This is a public matter. You have to recognize that. You can't take over another man's animals without permission. Think about it. You'd be going against your own traditions."

Abe, fierce-eyed, didn't answer. Lars Hamil merely grinned. Shawn Lynch, his voice as pleasant as could be, his brown eyes limpid, told Evan that they had thought about it and the matter was settled. "We're well within our rights," he added. Shawn's self-assurance ran bone deep, and for good reason: The Lynch tribe's bank accounts were reasonably healthy; two ranches were under Lynch ownership; cattle with the Mule Bit brand always seemed to come out of winter looking sleeker than any others.

Evan said, "Shawn, remember when you signed a transit permit for these sheep? These very animals you're looking at today?" He pointed to the pasture. "You too, Abe. And you, Lars. What's changed? I grant you that no one of you was full of joy about it, back then in August, but not one of you made a big hoop-de-doo, either."

That brought a few moments of silence. Evan used them to turn his attention to JT Timberlake. "What's changed, since then?" he asked.

Abe said, "You're way off the subject. This is cattle country, always has been. That's the main thing here. And this meeting is closed, Hughes. We've wrapped it up."

Evan nodded. "All right, Abe. I'll just add, for the record, that two sheep outfits grazed the Sagehen back around 1895 and -96. But never mind, we don't have to argue about that, it's simply a fact. Let me answer my own question, since nobody else wants to. The answer is this: Mr. Timberlake here, he's gone to work and he's got you ranchers all fired up. Now, tell me I'm wrong."

JT let out a harsh sound that was meant to be heard and he pushed forward and stepped into the little space in front of the porch and he poked a finger at Evan. "Look me in the eye when you say that."

"I'm looking."

"You're trying a diversion, and I don't like it."

"What are you so upset about, JT? Ashamed of your work?"

"Ashamed! Listen, BLM, nobody, least of all a federal bureaucrat..."

Abe Fox shouted, "Climb down, JT, he's trying to spook you."

Evan shrugged and kept quiet. He wanted JT to have a breather, gather his wits, and speak—and, just maybe, move himself out on a limb.

JT did just that. "I've expressed myself on these matters, if that's what you're getting at, Hughes. I've nothing to hide. As a landowner, I'm proud to take a stand, with others... my friends, who also live on the land and care for it." He paused, for reaction. All eyes were upon him. He would have appreciated some show of enthusiasm, a few yells, some "go-get-ums." He began again. "My sole purpose in being here, today, is to see that our way of life is not trampled on...."

Evan broke in. "Tell us about Far Haven. What kind of trampling do you take that to be?"

"What?"

"Don't play around, JT. We're grown men—and women. Everybody knows Far Haven is getting set to take pretty much all the lower Sagehen. I'm asking if you ever met with any of those people. I'm asking, for instance, if you ever had any talk with them about that big piece of grazing these sheep are headed for." Evan felt that, for once, he had made a forceful public statement. "I was winging it, though," he told himself. "Now he'll shoot me down."

But JT muffed it. "That's a mighty big question, full of innuendo. I'll ask you to rephrase it."

The crowd reacted, at last, with a few snickers. Sandra Fox stepped forward, to rescue JT. "Evan Hughes, what the hell's this got to do with anything here? We're opposing sheep on Sagehen grazing and we're on to you and Forest Service trying your best to set up precedents. That's the long and the short of it. You're dragging in other stuff."

"Bull's eye," Evan thought. "JT ought to take lessons." Yes, precedent. Precisely what he and Dave Darwin had been up to. Flexible land-management acts that might lead to more. Breaking trail. Pushing ecological judgments to the fore. Now it was Evan's turn to try a sidle. "I asked a question, Sandra. JT hasn't answered it."

She was having none of that. "Look, if you got questions, take them up with him. Don't go dragging us into it."

Shawn Lynch pronounced. "Sandra, you're absolutely right. Let's go home."

Lars Hamil opened his mouth, to second Shawn, but Winona Turpin had both hands up, jumping a little, trying to speak. Lars said, affectionately, "Go ahead, girl." He had known her since she was a baby.

She said, "Maybe these sheep aren't the problem."

Sandra was amazed. "Winona, what the hell?"

"Sandra, I mean, they *are* a problem, but maybe not the one we ought to be working on."

"Well, go ahead, what's on your mind?" It was as though the two women were speaking in private.

"Remember, last July, we all talked a lot about the DuckWing and how Far Haven had plans for an airport here? We talked about planes harassing the stock and what it might be like—jets coming in low, right over our houses? Then we quit, dropped the subject."

"What's the use of talk? There's nothing anybody can do about Far Haven."

Winona continued. "Then we watched Far Haven take the Warm Springs Ranch. They've got plans for some kind of spa up there. Then we watched them buy out the Peterson place. Like you said, there wasn't anything we could do. Some people kept saying it would all turn out for the best, anyway. And word came down about the hotel and alpine village and damming the river. Far Haven sure has been taking, and taking, and I'm saying their taking is a lot more serious, compared to a bunch of sheep. Someplace, out of sight, you can bet there's a great big master plan for the Sagehen, and you know what, Sandra? The OX could be next."

Vienna Hamil jumped up from where she'd been sitting on her heels, next to Lars. "Winona—dammit, what's come over you?"

Sandra hissed at Vienna, "Don't."

There was a pause, people staring hard at the women, or looking down at their feet, ashamed to be watching what appeared to be the tumble-down, right out here in the open, of twenty years of comradeship.

And Evan Hughes—he forgot about public policy. He leaned, body and mind, toward Winona Turpin; not because she was agreeing, in part, with him, but because she had taken a leap and was standing, for at least a few flustered moments, against the drift of things. And Evan spoke severely, to himself. "That terrific woman—she was in your office—you could have been getting acquainted. Instead, you talked cows. God, but you are a stiff stick, Hughes." But he was happy to be at the DuckWing, after all. "Che sarà, sarà," he thought, "and the devil take the hindmost." He stayed in that kind of daze for a while longer, hardly hearing JT's rash attempt to get back on stage. "Winona," he was saying, "you and I've known each other a good long time. I want to say, I appreciate…"

Sandra and Vienna turned on him. Vienna said, "You, shut up."

JT tried a grin and shrugged, as if to ask, "Ah well, what chance does a man have?"

Another silence, this time it was an expectation, a waiting for Ed Turpin, the man whose grown daughter had just gone against the grain so hard it seemed she might end up siding with the feds. Let Ed speak. But his dry mouth stayed crimped. This cowman whose rascally—no, downright mean-spirited—law-bending against BLM bureaucracy had earned him a certain standing—this man had, at the end, nothing to say. That was fitting, though. Ed Turpin had always been short on words, long on action. Abe Fox waggled his white eyebrows at his old friend. The two men stared at each other until the creases in Ed's face softened a little, sketched a smile.

"You figure this one out, Abe. I'm headed for Phoenix." He turned away and that acted as a signal. The meeting broke up.

Vienna went to Winona. They walked, arm in arm, into the side yard, for privacy; no one could tell for sure whether they were having it out or consoling each other. Sandra stayed with Abe, helping him rise from the porch steps.

Amos Snow appointed two OX hands to fix the pasture fence, pronto. "Nothing fancy, enough to hold through the night." Then he raised his voice. "Meet here, nine in the morning, all who are willing. Horseback."

A rancher from Jack Creek, far to the north, suggested ten o'clock might be better. Amos agreed, called out the change. "Ten, then. Sharp."

From the broad and happy face of Pancho Jones came a loud "Shi-it."

Amos asked, patiently, "What's wrong, Pancho?"

"Nothing, excepting we've all forgot how to fork a horse." He gave a shout of laughter, his belly jigged. Some cowhands laughed with him, some didn't, and everybody surged toward their vehicles.

Abe Fox took it slowly, not wanting to be jostled. He was pleased with the way the meeting had turned out. Too bad, though, about Winona. Wonderful girl. Abe would always think of her as the bouncy teenager who had made such a difference in the life of his beloved son; and it was pure hell to see her and the whole Turpin family sold out. Things were moving too fast. Abe and his people were being herded into sunset. Sure, the OX would stay and the Lynches' empire, maybe the Hamils, and three or four big sheep outfits up north: Donnadio and his crowd. They'd weather these gold mines and spasms of oil drilling, mineral prospecting, national defense demands, BLM interference, Far Haven schemes, whatever. But the small outfits would go under. Tragic is what that was. But a man had to adapt to progress. The saying lacked the bite of former years.

Chapter 25

THAT LONG DAY at the DuckWing, dwindling, not yet done.

Bryan Lashley, walking toward his horse, heard Jaimie Dellums yell, for all to hear, "Sheeper, where you think you're going?"

Lashley didn't turn, didn't stop. He growled, "If it's any of your business, I've a horse to take care of."

"Forget it, Sheeper. You and me have got something to finish."

Amos went to Jaimie. "No, that's all over with."

Jaimie sneered and spit on the ground, but Amos kept talking. "There's things need doing. You're in charge here, I realize that. See that those guys fix the fence, would you? Keep an eye on the sheep, of course—whatever you think is necessary."

Amos's words weren't right; they were off by a hair; they weren't quite man-to-man. Jaimie wouldn't take them; not today, not here, in front of half the town, half the valley. "Listen, Amos. First off, I'll do what all of you are too chickenshit to do." He spun away and ran into the house.

Pancho Jones said, "What do you suppose he's up to, in there?"

Bryan Lashley resumed his walk. Amos called to him. "Lashley? Do I have the name right? I'd be obliged if you'd ride on out of here, before there's more trouble."

"No, I'll stay with my sheep."

"Well, that's what I mean. You can't do that. Sagehen people will be taking care of these animals, tomorrow."

Lashley was in enemy territory, but he said what had to be said. "Uh huh, I know how that goes. You Sagehen people will *care* the sheep to death—lots of ways to lose sheep, along the way."

"Nobody said anything like that."

"Didn't have to." He gave Amos a grim smile.

And Evan Hughes gave himself another bad mark, for not having guessed what Donnadio's herder had just made plain. Amos Snow's failure to come back with a quick, vigorous denial cinched it.

And now all the talking had, at last, come to an end. The house door slammed. Jaimie Dellums stood on the porch holding his rifle at port arms. He bounded down the steps, trotted across the yard, braced himself against a fence post and snapped a cartridge into the chamber. Amos ran at him, followed by Evan Hughes. The rifle barked and a ewe went down. Jaimie put a hand on the post and neatly vaulted the fence. He lost his hat, but kept the rifle.

The ewe was stretched out on her side, kicking. A long, bleating scream came from her. She drew a shuddering breath and screamed again.

Parents herded children toward the road. A few ranchers and cowhands thought of dashing to their pickups to grab racked rifles, but none of them went. None of them wanted to miss the walkdown—two very angry men, Amos Snow and Evan Hughes, stalking Jaimie Dellums, barehanded.

The first to reach the dying animal was Flora Kimball. Bryan Lashley came next. He tugged a big clasp knife from his pocket, said to Flora, "Now, watch yourself." He put a booted foot on one of the ewe's hind feet while he held her muzzle hard against his own leg. He slashed at her neck. Bright blood spurted across his knife and hand. The ewe gave a descending series of burbly sighs as she stiffened and died.

Winona was there, hugging Flora. "Come on, kiddo, let's get out here." She tried to lift her away, but Flora, dry-eyed and mute, laid her body across the ewe's body. Winona couldn't budge her.

Horace Giles, circling Amos and Evan, called to Jaimie, "I'm with you."

Lashley stood. He saw Jaimie backing slowly into the pasture. He saw Jack at the north side, calmly loping alongside a run of sheep. He saw that Jaimie had noticed Jack. The rifle rose, to track the dog. Lashley made three great leaps and crashed into Jaimie. They both went down, as the rifle looped away toward Giles, who made a shoestring catch and straightened, triumphant. Jaimie bounded to his feet, begging, "Horace, toss it here, quick, toss it here."

Horace obeyed. Jaimie caught and swung to meet Lashley's next rush. Lashley rose into a crouch. He looked squarely into the rifle's muzzle and the face of a man who—Lashley knew it for absolute fact—had crossed the line.

The DuckWing scene flicked into stop-motion. Even the sheep were beginning to calm down. Only a rifle spoke. It wasn't Jaimie's. Jaimie seemed to have turned suddenly languid, undecided. He was falling.

Lashley's horse pricked its ears eastward. A moment later, Sagehen citizens found the same direction, but everything looked normal up there, brushy slopes quiet, low skyline of the Heeaws fading in a pale sunset color, but then came motion: a horse, galloping, a rider, bent low.

Someone said, "John Moss."

"You're right," someone else said. "That's Brownie, I'd know that horse anywhere."

Those were the first words heard by Sheriff Pierre Labray as he and Bull Hogan came up the driveway. "Here we go again," he said.

Both lawmen tried to go blank on the man writhing on the pasture ground. What could be done for him was being done, by at least a dozen people. "Bull," Labray said, "first thing I want to impress on you is, we've had it with John Moss. This time we take him—the hard way."

"I guess," said Bull.

"What d'you mean, you guess?"

"I don't know, Pierre. Wouldn't have believed it of John, that's all. He's a joker type, not a dry-gulcher."

"You got eyes don't you? What's the matter?"

Bull had eyes, he was using them, picking scenes from the turmoil: Jaimie Dellums being carried to a van that had been driven into the yard; a woman dashing out of the house with what looked like dish towels; a woman who looked quite dead, lying on top of a dead sheep; a saddled horse tied to a fence post. "Pierre, I'll take that black horse there."

"All right. I'll settle with the owner. I see there's a saddle gun. Use it, if you have to."

Labray stomped back through the crowd and leaned into the cruiser to patch through a call to his other deputy. "Whatever you're doing, drop it. Get on down here to the DuckWing."

Bull huffed and puffed to the fence, taking plenty of advice along the way. A young man had untied the horse. Bull held out his hand, ready to say "Thanks." But the young man was Henry Izard and he was climbing aboard and this time there was no clumsy turning and clattering on Blackrock asphalt. The black horse broke away into a clean lope.

Bull roared at Henry, but he didn't waste time running after the horse, the way some were doing. He put his big hands on his big hips and bellowed. "Get me a horse. You cowpokes, you cow people, Jesus Christ, move it! Get me one goddamn horse."

Land blurred past, bright saltbush tones and medium shades of sage, a prickly carpet under a darkening sky. Henry was afraid, but felt no uncertainty. He wasn't tagging after a man, he was man-hunting, but he wasn't alone: Jaimie's agony, his low, animal sounds; the humanlike cries of the gut-shot sheep; Flora's collapse—all of these rode with him, into a crazed and dusky new world—none of it like paperbacks, none of it.

The horse broke stride at a cutbank, danced cleverly along the rim, found a crossing and took the next long and gradual slope, slowed to a walk near the crest. Brownie stood on the next swell of ground, watching his back trail, his ears pointed at the steps of a horse that he knew.

John Moss was on foot, to the left of Brownie. Henry reached for the saddle gun, pulled it and found it utterly familiar, the very model of his brother's lever action Winchester, an ancient thing, and reassuring. The black horse walked steadily forward.

John Moss raised both hands as Henry rode up. He grinned. "You taking me in?"

"You shot a man, from cover."

"How is he? How is Jaimie?"

"I don't know." He guided the black horse closer to Brownie. The gun scabbard was empty.

John said, "It's over there." He pointed. "See? Against that sage. I saved you the trouble. We don't want any accidents—not between you and me, Henry."

"You're up to something."

"No. I'd like you to take charge of that rifle. It's not been fired. Evidence, for the sheriff." He lowered his hands to his belt. "I didn't shoot Jaimie."

"Don't lie to me."

John liked Henry's tone, as well as the words: straight, no holding back. "Henry, a man has to have motivation to shoot a person. Wouldn't you agree?"

"Or be crazy."

"Fair enough. Now, you can call me a no-account cowman, a person with poor judgment, and you could be right. But you know I am not a crazy man. What happened back there—Brownie and I, we put on a diversion."

Henry believed it, relief swept him. "I'm listening," he said.

"I'll give you the whole story, start to finish. Damn, I sure could use a cigarette about now."

"You quit."

"So I did. You think Jaimie won't make it?"

"I told you, I don't know."

John sat down, dug his boot heels into the ground and propped his elbows on his knees. He talked, about the blizzard and the quiet few days travel in the Heeaws, about meeting with the sheepmen, the drive and the break in the fence. "That was the one piece of bad luck. Bryan went down to talk our way out of it. He and Jaimie got in a fight, but Manny and I kept cool, stayed out of sight, waited to see if Bryan handled it, and he did. We waited out that boring cowmen's conference, watched the whole Sagehen pour in. When Jaimie comes busting out of the house and shoots a sheep, that's when Manny gets his own rifle and lies down prone. You know the rest."

"That was dumb, firing downhill, all those people."

"He had motivation, Henry. That's what I'm trying to point out to you. See, Manny and Bryan are friends. Manny's a suspicious cuss, and proud. Well, him and me, we treated each other all right. With Bryan, though— a whole different matter. Bryan and Manny are friends. The point is, Henry, friend is a strong thing."

"So, Manny takes a chance of killing some innocent person."

"You put it that way it sounds pretty bad, but I guess that's the size of it—plus the possibility Manny is a deadeye shot. I don't know about that."

"Why'd you put yourself out for him?"

John laughed. "Come on, Henry, that's easy. Remember? I'm seriously concerned about crowds taking a hand in things. After he shot Jaimie, Manny went to his horse and all he said to me was, 'John, they can have me, back at the ranch. Not here.'"

"Yeah," Henry said. "I see what you mean." He stepped down and offered the Winchester. "Trade you."

"No, that's all right. It's Bryan's. When you see Bryan, give him my regards. And he might be in need of some help about now."

"What about you, John? Where you headed?"

"I don't rightly know. Out of here, for now—got some figuring to do—straighten my head out."

Henry plucked John's rifle from the sage bush and rammed it into the black horse's scabbard.

John asked, "Don't you want to sniff it?"

"Let the sheriff do it." They grinned at each other.

John said, "Well, I'd best get a move on." He went to Brownie and took the reins. He mounted, then leaned down. "You take care of yourself, pardner."

"You too." They shook hands.

Henry climbed awkwardly into the saddle, holding the Winchester in one hand. He heard Brownie's fast walk, noisy in brittle saltbush and dry sage.

Chapter 26

 THE PHONE RANG, in Jerry Haun's living room. It was Winona, worried about Flora. "She's disappeared. I assumed she'd gone home with somebody else, but I've called all over."

"Good Lord, something might have happened."

"Jerry, that's why I'm calling. I feel awful. I should have stayed with her, at that dead sheep. She wouldn't listen to anybody. Then the shooting and—I wasn't thinking straight today—when I looked for her, later on, she wasn't there. Simply gone, without a word to me."

"Winona, we have to find her."

"I'm trying to think back to what she might have done. I was so distracted today—God, you should have seen—after we took care of Jaimie a couple cowboys got to bad-mouthing the herder and that turned into a fight. Evan Hughes and some others jumped in to stop it. Naturally, the whole thing was a mess—nobody could tell the bad guys from the good guys. Labray got so upset he went around firing his pistol over their heads, to get their attention. You know, he's got this reputation of never having to use his gun... well, today he used it."

Terrible images confronted Jerry. The town had been full of wild talk. "I'll start at the DuckWing," he said. He didn't wait for her reply.

The house was dark, not a single vehicle in sight. One yard light made the two dogs look like pale green spectres. Neither dog barked. They watched Jerry walk to the fence—one dog near the barn, the other at the house. The sheep were quiet, except for barely audible sounds of life, as from a single living thing whose furthest bounds were lost in the night beyond the cast of the yard light. Jerry noticed that the main barn door, on hangers, wasn't quite closed. As he walked to the barn the black-and-white dog came up to him, sniffed at his trousers and followed him, into warm spaciousness and stale, cobwebby smells that made Jerry stop for a moment, taken by memories—the barns and potato sheds of Idaho.

"Jerry?"

He walked the center aisle, slowly, his eyes adjusting. "How did you know it was me?"

"I don't know, I just did." Flora sat cross-legged on a thick spread of hay, next to a stack of bales. She said, "See, I made myself a bed."

"Yes, well..."

"I decided to stay the night. I was crazy there, for a while. In the morning I'll let the sheep out."

"I'm glad you're OK. People are worried. Winona called."

"She and I have fallen out. We're so different, but we're still friends, I hope. I guess friends can fall out, can't they?"

Jerry's vision had adjusted, he was shocked at Flora's disheveled appearance. The perfection on display at the drug store was gone. He sat on a hay bale and put his hands on his knees.

She said, "Bats hang out here, I saw them."

"They don't bother you?"

"Not yet. And don't tell me I have a special thing for animals." She laughed. "Vince has some strange ideas about Flora. So do you. So do I. It's funny... when I'm with Vince, he talks; when I'm with you, I talk."

"Talk all you want, Flora; I'm just glad you're OK."

"Yes, you said that."

Jack walked down the aisle and plunked down next to Flora. She said, "I'm leaving Sagehen, tomorrow. That reminds me, I'll have to ask you to get my back pay for me. Jerry, do you think you'll work at the pharmacy until you can draw Social Security?"

"It's not likely."

"Really?"

"Hard to tell."

"I admire how you stay so levelheaded. You should've seen me today, made a total, ugly fool of myself. I upset Winona, too. That woman, she's so gutsy... she told JT a thing or two... but when I was with that sheep, the dead one, I think I disgusted Winona. Really, I think so. She's gotten on my nerves, too, the last few days. We were irksome to each other. 'Irksome,' that's what Gramma used to say, one of her favorite words. My gramma raised me. And an aunt, they both worked at it. Dad died overseas. My mom died after bringing me into this world."

"Your grandmother," he said, "in Twin Falls, on your father's side."

"You know all that?"

"You told me."

"I suppose I did, more than once." She laughed and reached to Jack and rubbed behind his ears. "I wonder what his name is. Hey, lovely dog, what's your name?"

Jerry said, "I like your talking, I like it a lot."

"You never said... well, tell you what, I'll give you the true story about that day down at John Moss's. Want to hear it?"

"Sure."

"You let us off at the cattle guard, right? I told you not to bother to come pick us up."

"I wondered about that."

"Yes, I imagine you did. I was burning bridges and not admitting it, scared to take a stand. So, after Winona and I rode out from John's, I broke down and cried... looked up into Wild Horse canyon and simply howled. Winona didn't fuss at me, she just got down off Brownie and said, 'Let's take a walk.' She started picking flowers. We ended up making this huge wreath, not for any reason, just something to do while I spilled my guts. Winona listened, that's about all she did. When I got around to saying, 'I'm going to Blackrock, right this minute,' she said, 'Let's go.'"

"It's strange," he said, "the way things work out."

She thought, "Now he'll tell me it's time to go home."

He said, "You need some blankets. Is the house locked?"

"I wouldn't know."

Without a word, he got up and went into the yard. The other dog came forward to escort him to the porch. The door wasn't locked. Jerry found a light switch and tiptoed into the kitchen, which was a mess. The other rooms were neat as a pin. Someone had stripped Jaimie's bed for wrappings for the trip to the hospital, but there were two cotton blankets on a closet shelf. Jerry took them. Back in the barn, he spread them over Flora.

"Thanks," she said. "Jerry, can I tell about my gramma?"

"Sure." He sat on his hay bale and listened. After a while his eyes closed. Flora's voice was a faraway murmur, Jerry was remembering. It was almost as though Gramma Kimball spoke.

Elise Kimball, devout Mormon, born in Ogden, reared in Twin Falls. Her forebears on both sides made the great trek to the place that had been promised. Elise spent most of her working life in stores, clerking, managing. She was orthodox, her moral view usually to the fore, no one escaped it. But she loved to praise Twin Falls, especially its glory years when there had been a real downtown. Slow traffic, narrow streets and people coming in from all across the plains, from sugar beet and potato farms, irrigated produce farms, crossroads places—and the wide world came too, passengers getting on and off the Union Pacific, right there in town. Winters were hard—mean winds, sooty frost that took your breath away. Indoors—dimestores, department stores, all the retail places—crowded and perfumed, cheap candy, a block of solid milk chocolate for two pennies, crepe paper decor, wooden tables loaded with cloth goods and hardware and trinkets. Farm women told Elise, "Without the town, we'd die."

Flora stopped. Jerry knew she was waiting, as she always did, hoping for a trade. This time he would try as never before, he would not deny her. He kept his eyes shut. A few words loosed others, they tumbled. Burley and Boise and Salt Lake and Winnemucca. He stopped. He wondered if she had fallen asleep. He said, "Flora, you've seen a lot more places than I have. Did you ever count them?"

"Count? You want me to make a list?"

"Sure."

She began. The intervals between towns lengthened. She said, "I'm too tired."

He stood and she said, "Don't go."

"It's late, you need to rest, been a hard day."

She sat up, quickly. Jack lifted his head. She said, "I like being with you. I like it a lot."

He was amazed. How easy, after all, to kneel on the hay, to go to her. She threw off the blankets and her breath was near enough to fan his cheek as she whispered, "I'm taking my shoes off." They fumbled with laces. Flora tossed her shoes into the darkness and one of them happened to hit Jack. He jumped up. Flora, and then Jerry, fussed over him. Their hands strayed from his sleek fur to each other and they lay back and Jack twitched his ears, yawned tremendously and settled into a half doze, listening to night sounds.

Chapter 27

 AT TEN O'CLOCK Ed Turpin turned off the TV and headed for bed, passing by his daughter who was still hunched over the phone table, trying to locate Flora. Ed paused. "Leave it for morning," he said.

She looked up from the phone book, startled by his words; they came out of the past, from life on the TN. Morning, the Goddess; they all knew her. She was the one called upon when a day's work unraveled. At sundown on such a day you had to simplify, step back, wait for sunup. She said, "OK, Dad."

In the kitchen, Florence doggedly packed equipment into beer cartons. Winona watched, aching with tiredness. "Mom, quit that. I'll make us some hot chocolate."

They sat at the table. Florence wanted to hear, all over again, the complex DuckWing story, one that was yet to play itself to an ending. Winona covered only parts of it. After a while Winona realized her mother's thoughts were elsewhere. She was pushing a finger, lightly, around certain whorls of woodgrain that she knew by heart. The table had come from the workshop of Ed's father. A photo tacked at the end of the cupboard showed him and four other Turpins posed between the foreheads of saddle horses: a sister and a brother, both frowning; the mother, peering from under the flop brim of a felt hat in a deliberately redneck manner; the father, shoulders back, a firm hand on a bridle; the grandfather, the only one with a smile. Florence reminded herself to not leave that photo behind. She pointed to it. "Amazing, how I've had it there without a frame, all these years, letting it curl and get flyspecked. Look, your hair was cropped close then, like now."

"Yup, full circle."

"You were a pesky handful. All the scrapes, it's a wonder—remember the bears?"

"How could I forget? You told me, about a hundred times."

Out of a lush streamside patch of black currants, a bear cub had tumbled into sunshine in front of a towheaded girl. The cub's mother rose up, tall and sudden, from behind a down tree. The family dog yelped his head off, staying one quick jump behind the little girl.

Florence said, "We were lucky the dog was with us. Which one was it?"

"I was only four, Mom. Dozer?"

"Yes, it was Dozer. My memory's shot to hell." She tipped her cup, studied it critically, let it settle back onto a wet circle. "I used to use saucers. Even when I had people in for a quick lunch, sometimes I'd get out the china. I put cream into a fancy little pitcher, a blue one, it's gone now. I laid out a tablecloth, the whole shebang. There was a time when I knew how to put on the dog."

"Mom, you were in the Brown Palace once, weren't you?"

"Oh yes, big stock show in Denver. We had us a time. That was before you kids came." She glanced away and drew a decisive breath, and Winona knew what was coming. Mom would make the effort now, time being so short—only a handful of days before the Mayflower van showed up. Some kind of reconciliation had to be in sight before she would allow herself to go to Phoenix. "Dad was thinking about us," she said, "when he sold to Smoke Creek."

"Sure, Mom."

"He was trying his best, arranging financial security for all of us. I wouldn't have agreed, that's why he up and did it. Winona, can't you say something to him, some little thing? He's your father, he loves you."

Winona held her cup with both hands, thought dark thoughts about the old knothead, her father, the man who could not bring himself to allow a lifelong partner, his wife, to have a say in the big decision. What on earth could he have been thinking? That after he was gone, that partner would not be able to face reality? That woman who was as smart as they come? Damn his hide, he knows that. Mom, who's decided a thousand things her man didn't even know about, or had forgotten. Tough decisions, many of them. Sick kids, randy cowboys, cranky animals. As for the daughter, Dad gave her even less thought. She'd find herself a man—that was the A to Z of it. The hell of it all was that Mom always did what she was doing now, standing up for her man, keeping the family tight, the only way she knew. It couldn't be any different. "OK, Mom. Don't worry any more about this, OK? Dad and me'll pardner along, some damn way."

Florence leaned across the big table to touch her daughter, her eyes tearful. "I know how you felt, about the ranch."

Winona got up and rounded the table and gave Florence a quick hug. That was all. There would be no more talk about this. In spite of her years on the coast, Winona was still a Turpin: a few words when necessary, swallow what you had to, get on with the work.

Florence rinsed the cups. Winona said, "I'll take a walk, to the road and back."

"The flashlight's on the peg."

She didn't take the flashlight. She knew every foot of the way. At the county road she leaned on the brace of the gatepost. TN fencing receded into invisibility, north and south and west. She thought about strangers taking over. Bulldozers and earthmovers. She thought about the very near future. What were her chances, a woman with cowhand skills and no land and no man?

The low-lying river meadows made, as usual, a night space blacker than any other, and tonight it was filled with unseen presences. A stranger, someone from outside, would know nothing about those. Winona tried to visualize a Far Haven planner or surveyor or builder—or a condo buyer—through their eyes. She tried to make everything go away and rise up fresh, the way those other folks might see it: sky and mountains and pools of valley darkness and the sprinkle of town lights—and she felt that she succeeded, for a moment or two, then all was normal again, but in that little jump, that gap, she thought she had looked into her country without being of it.

She stepped into the dry irrigation ditch and walked to the main headgate that controlled flows in any combination of three directions. She had rebuilt it, only a few months ago. She leaned against it, inched her attention along the blackness of the Jedediahs, the down-jags and the upthrusts that blocked out stars. A lightness came, an exhilarating shucking of responsibility. She played the stranger again, for all he and she were worth and the Sagehen recreated itself, tumultuously, seemed to shake itself, and then it settled, remaining as mysterious, as luxurious as ever. What had she found? A scary freedom. Owning nothing, she had it all.

She climbed out of the ditch and ducked through the fence and walked north along the road. Everything was ordinary again and she was very tired, but something had happened and she would have to tell. Winona, no solitaire, needed a confidant. Who might it be? Finally, she smiled.

Chapter 28

 A FEW MINUTES before dawn. Flora walked out of the barn into a bright morning. Jerry still slept. The big, brown dog raised his head; he had been dozing on trampled ground in front of the back porch. The black-and-white dog stood like a statue, near the fence, watching the sheep that were beginning to raise their voices. "That's what woke me up," Flora said. She went to the southwest corner of the pasture, found the main gate, a clever contraption made of dump rake wheels bound and braced against each other by taut baling wire. It opened easily. A few sheep noticed, but they were uncertain; they waited on each other. Finally, one ewe took the lead and behind her came a few more and then the flow. Jack followed, casually, happily. Once, he stopped and looked back at Flora.

The band moved at a good speed across poor grazing. It crossed the county road. There was a pileup and a spreading in two directions along a fence. The left prong prevailed; the entire band moved south, crossed Fox Road, into unfenced meadowland where it slowed and spread toward the river, its woolly backside catching the first rays of the new sun.

Flora returned to the yard. She heard sounds from inside the house. Footsteps on linoleum, she recognized them. She stepped into the porch, opened the inner door. Jerry stood at the kitchen counter, watching a percolator. He turned and smiled, but his glance didn't quite meet hers. She forgave him.

"I'm starved," she said. "Is there any bread?"

"I don't know. There's a toaster."

She rummaged, found bread and butter and jam. She loaded the toaster and watched the play of distortions in the shiny curved chrome. The toaster popped. "It's a beautiful day," she said.

"Sure is." He poured coffee.

"What about the blankets?"

"I put them back."

"Good."

They ate, standing up. They rinsed the cups and the percolator. Flora said, "This whole kitchen needs a going over."

"Yes."

They went outside. The brown dog came up to them. "I suppose he's hungry," Flora said.

"Where's the other dog?"

She pointed. "Gone, with the sheep."

He stared at the empty pasture. "Good Lord, I didn't even notice."

"I turned the sheep loose, like I said I would."

"Yes."

"I better get out of here."

"Where do you want to go?" He reached into a pocket to make sure he had the Toyota keys.

"I don't want to be—dropped off—anywhere." She nearly believed that last night had been a dream. "He'll never change," she thought.

"I'll drive you any place you want to go, Flora. You name it."

"I'll take a walk, with the sheep, maybe. Goshen, maybe."

"You can't walk to Goshen. Come on, I'll drive you there."

"Yes, I can." She was too angry, too disappointed, to say more. She walked away, into the driveway. She tossed her hair the way she always did when things had gone wrong.

He watched her go. The old misery, the old histories, rose through his body, turned him rigid. But he took a step toward the Toyota, two steps, three—he was in motion. He stopped at the Toyota only long enough to grab the title and insurance card from the glove compartment. He left the key in the ignition. Somebody might drive the car to a safe place, hold it for him. Somebody might steal it. Small matters. He slammed the door.

Flora heard that. She waited for the motor to turn over. Instead, she heard Jerry's footsteps on the driveway, hurried steps. He was running!

They caught up with the sheep and walked among them and came to the river and stood on hummocky ground, watching dark swirls of water, listening to lappings and gurglings.

Flora said, "What about the Toyota? They'll think you did it."

"Did what?"

"Turned the sheep loose."

He puzzled over that; it hadn't entered his mind. "Well, so what? Besides, these sheep aren't going anywhere. Look at them, stuffing themselves, happy as—I don't know what."

"Yes. Silly of me. I had this notion that when I opened the gate they'd go off and, you know—escape."

"Don't worry about them, Flora."

They walked downstream, getting their feet wet, snagging their clothing on dead willow stubs and picking up loads of dew from the lush vegetation. Jack, from higher ground, watched them go.

They passed the first of the Spring Gulch rapids, about fifty yards of turmoil, dark in cliff shadows, the footing along the bank so narrow that they couldn't avoid the spray tossed from the wave crests. The next two rapids were not as wild, and then the river took a long, lazy swing west.

Jerry knelt on a rock that shelved into the river. He took off his glasses and scooped handfuls of water to drink, to throw on his face, to clean his glasses. He polished the glasses with a handkerchief, facing upstream into a blur of scenery. He put the glasses on and the top lines of the Jedediahs leaped into sharp focus. The lower slopes were hidden by the intervening hills that closed off the southern reaches of the Sagehen valley.

He remembered his first day in the Sagehen—driving south from Monax, job-hunting. Early morning fog, the fog lifting, slowly and raggedly to reveal and conceal until the entire Jedediah range loomed over him— aloof, asking nothing—giving nothing—uncaring beauty. He had stopped the car. Another car honked in passing. He looked at his watch. Twenty minutes had passed. He was late for his interview with Vincent Van Horn.

He turned away, with no regrets, only wonder. Flora was walking back from the riverside. Water dripped from her face. "I lost my comb," she said.

"Use mine, if you want."

"OK."

They sat on the ground. He watched her tug at her hair. "I have to tell her," he thought. "It has to be now." He said, "I stole ninety thousand dollars, from JT Timberlake."

"What?"

"I did, really."

She laughed. "This I don't believe." But she believed. He had opened a conversation, he was letting her in on something serious. She was mightily pleased.

He told her all, leaving out only one important fact: the name of his co-conspirator. "What do you think?" he asked.

"Who'd ever have thought—Jerry Haun, of all people."

He lay back, looked into the sky. Four words: who'd ever have thought. They burned, they cut, and they didn't matter. But he had no way of speaking about that—impossible. He shut his eyes against sun glare. The day had turned hot. He looked at his watch. Eleven thirty. Where had the morning gone?

Flora condemned herself. She gripped Jerry's comb so hard its teeth made dents in her hand. But then she turned stubborn. It was his turn to speak. She'd wait until hell froze over, she was not going to be the first to speak. And would this clamming-up, by him, by her, turn everything bad—the being with the sheep, the walk along the river, last night's wanton creatures of the dark? She risked a glance at him. He was smiling. It was a grim one, but there it was.

He repeated the question. "What do you think?"

"It doesn't matter a whit, to me. I mean, I think it's just the greatest rip-off—maybe wrong—oh hell, it's all blood money, anyway."

He sat up. Blood money, exactly what Ruth Zalent had called it. He laughed. He looked Flora full in the face, laughing, showing the inside of his mouth. A gold filling flashed. He turned away, struggled to contain himself, but he kept bubbling. His shoulders shook. He took a handkerchief from his pocket and wiped tears from his eyes. "Good Lord," he said.

They wouldn't make Blackrock until nightfall, if then. They were in desert country now, a land dominated by greasewood. They came to low cliffs, bastions of a small mesa, and a swale—shallow patches of slowly moving water no more than three or four inches deep, and shallow muck hosting bright green plants. They drank. The only shade worthy of the name was under an overhang that was split by high, deep, slanting crevices crammed with branches and spines and bleached bones. A wood-rat castle.

They looked out from there, into the dazzle. Flora leaned back against rock, arched her breasts against her sheep-blooded, unfresh blouse.

"Can you imagine me," she said, "at the store, behind the counter, like this?"

He closed his eyes and hugged her. They went to the ground, their hunger overriding with ease the heat and the powerful stink of wood rat.

Chapter 29

 BY EARLY MORNING the news had touched the farthest reaches of the valley: Jaimie Dellums was out of danger, would limp for the rest of his life; Donnadio's herder, injured in the free-for-all at the DuckWing, was in the hospital; the cattlemen's sheep drive would go ahead as scheduled.

Very few townspeople jumped into their cars to dash to the DuckWing, that morning, the way they'd done the day before. Many of them felt shame at having stood around watching and exposing their children to danger. Today, men on horseback; and it looked as though they had a wide field of play; intervention by the law probably would be late and minimal, partly because Sheriff Labray and Bull Hogan, mad as hornets and reinforced by state troopers, were busy hunting the gunman who'd downed Jaimie.

Also, local authorities had been confused by the rumor of a communique from Washington, JT Timberlake taking the credit for pulling the right string in Congress.

Yet another reason was the disarray among Forest Service and BLM people, what with the BLM's certified environmentalist, Evan Hughes, in jail with a slew of cowboys. That wouldn't do much for Hughes' clout vis-a-vis his superiors, on this particular day. And this particular day most likely would be the one that settled things.

Ruth Zalent, in the laundromat, listened to conversations. She was downcast, at first, gave herself a lecture about unrealistic hopes. Then she went right ahead and concocted another scheme, knowing that it was even flimsier than the last one. She rationalized it in her usual way: better than doing nothing. That was her great fear: doing nothing. She had winter in view, long evenings in the gold mine's throb, the entertainment of regrets.

She needed a phone. She walked to the drugstore. It was locked. The fluorescents were on, inside, but only in back. The clock behind the front checkout showed ten after eight. The only other public phone in town was the broken one at Will's Garage. Ruth hurried half a block south, to the Yarbidge building, and went into Sagebrush Faction.

Henry Izard hunched over his Shredded Wheat and honey, his left hand holding open a textbook. Last night he'd been unable to study and he couldn't concentrate this morning, either, what with his mother restlessly pacing around the house. And now she was on the phone. He scowled and shut the book and watched his mother's shadow on the wall of the next room. Her voice had risen. "I don't care about that—no—yes—I see that, but what earthly use—I won't go out there and beg..." A long pause. Henry went into the bathroom and brushed his teeth. When he returned to pick up his book his mother was at the sink, still in her blue robe. She looked into the yard, a bemused expression on her face.

She turned to Henry. "I'm going with Ruth Zalent to the DuckWing."

He said, "You better stay away from there."

She sighed. "You forgot your juice, again." She went to the fridge. "So, you know where I'll be—maybe all day."

"DuckWing."

"Yup." She poured juice for both of them. He chug-a-lugged his and rinsed his glass and clunked it loudly onto the counter. "I don't imagine those guys need any more help."

"Ruth's idea is, they need help to do the right thing. Sort of show them the way. We plan to drive the sheep down-river and across to the Barrows' grazing, where they were supposed to go."

"That's just crazy, Mom."

"It's a thing to try." Belle was watching her son, closely, and was happy to see him giving some thought to what she was saying.

He grinned and shoved his book and papers into his cloth carrying bag. He shook his head. "Mom, you don't know the first thing about sheep."

"It so happens, I do."

"Huh?"

"Red and me. You and Brent hadn't come along yet. We helped a neighbor put sheep through the dip. Two or three times we did that. Henry, you'll miss your bus, and I have to get dressed." She went into her bedroom. Henry stayed where he was, puzzled, beginning to worry.

Belle came back, dressed in blue jeans, plaid shirt and sneakers. Her hair was swept back in a ponytail. She took a jacket from the hook on the back door. "Now then, what did I forget? Lunch? Not time enough."

Henry said, "It's dangerous."

She crossed the kitchen and sat down next to him. "Hell with the bus," she thought. "Damned yellow monster." She said, "Dad's gone off on another manhunt. Why? Why not wait till that herder shows up someplace? Why all this galloping around? Don't you talk 'dangerous' to me, young man. Why did you go galloping off after John Moss? No, not now—tell me later. And why did the sheriff have to make such a big chase out of it? A bunch of foolishness."

He nodded; that encouraged her. She dropped her guard, spoke about a husband who couldn't live without adventures. Marriage to such a man was not all sweet petunias. She reminded Henry of the size of the Izard family's annual income, not big enough to feed a saddle horse through long winters. And now they had two of the damned animals. She talked about Brent, her eldest. He had turned into a man too quickly. Thank God, he had survived it. And her younger son? The sensible one? He'd broken a man out of jail and gone gallivanting around the country with a man everybody knew was a cowboy trickster, and then he brings home another hay burner. That wasn't enough; last night he swipes a horse out from under the nose of the law and rides off hell-bent-for-Texas on his own stupid manhunt. That could have turned serious.

"It didn't turn out bad," he said.

"That's not the point. Look, do you have the foggiest notion of what it's like, waiting for men to come home?"

He began to answer, she stopped him. She was fierce. "Henry, I know there's your side of it. I know there's John Moss's side, and Dad's. What I'm saying to you is *my* side. You better be listening."

He nodded, his lips parted, he was looking into his mother's burning eyes, wanting to say something, but she hadn't finished. "Right now, this very minute, Dad is some place in the Heeaws, or wherever; we don't know what's going on, out there."

"You trying to scare me?"

"Maybe."

"Jeez, the heck with that. I can't sit down there in Goshen Central all day worrying about Dad, and you."

"I know you can't, but you will." She got up abruptly and went to the entryway and found a floppy gardening hat. She held it at arm's length, cocked her head. "Oh, well." She put it on.

Henry said, "There's cliffs along the Spring Gulch rapids. You'll be driving the sheep that way. I mean, that'll be the quickest. But there's places where the water comes close to the cliffs."

"Oh, dear. I didn't think of that."

"Brent and me and some kids ran the rapids in inner tubes."

"I'm glad I didn't know about it. What time of year?"

"School was out. July, maybe."

"The water will be lower now, there might be more space along the shore. What do you think?"

"There might be. Mom, I'll go with you."

"No you don't. Ladies' day." She glanced at the clock. "Try for the bus, you might make it."

Ruth Zalent put down the phone. Beth Schlegel looked up from her work bench. "I couldn't help hearing your half of the conversation."

"Oh, no problem. After all, it's your phone. And thanks."

Beth was in one of her down moods. Linder was due back from a Salt Lake art show, tomorrow. She had missed him more than was reasonable. She had been staring at her drafting board, criticizing into near nonexistence a design for a madrone-wood medallion. Ruth Zalent's excited talk about a sheep drive caught Beth's fancy. The word *drive*, a power word. She was tantalized, saw herself making something happen. She said, "I've half a mind to shut up shop and go with you."

"Why don't you? Three would certainly be better than two." But Ruth was in a terrible hurry and showed it, and she had doubts about this hefty young woman in a tight, purple turtleneck, flowing skirt, bare feet in leather thongs, slinky hair all over her shoulders.

Beth guessed all of that, but she smiled. "I can be ready in three minutes."

"Ruth, slow down," Belle said. "Better stop." She pointed into the meadows south of Fox Road. "Big surprise."

Ruth parked on the shoulder, near the east bank of the river. "Looks like somebody else had the same idea," she suggested. "Or maybe the sheep broke out on their own."

They got out of the car and looked for men and horses. "Just a dog," Beth said.

Belle said, "Let's get on with it."

They ran across hummocky ground, dodged around and under willows; then they were among the animals—shoals of them, clots, long drifts. Smelly, thick bodies, heads doggedly down. Ever-questing, nibbling lips. Beth felt surrounded by unseemly urgency and she didn't like it, but when they began the drive—running, shouting—liking became irrelevant.

As soon as Jack sensed the intent of the noises and wavings of the new herders, he went into action. In a few minutes he had the ragged edges at the north and east shaped up, but there was no forward movement.

Belle saw the problem: sheep were reluctant to move into the narrow passage between the river and rough high ground on the east. Instead, some of them had begun to eddy back, toward the county road. Belle ran that way, hoping the dog would help. And Jack did, racing past Belle to turn the renegades. Now the band was nicely compacted. Belle squinted, looking for action in the south, and there was some—a tentative dribble, agonizingly slow, hesitant.

Ruth had noticed a different motion. She yelled, "Here they come, men on horseback!"

Belle stood on tiptoe, but a patch of willows blocked her view. She yelled, "How far? How many?"

"At least two dozen, coming out of the yard at the DuckWing. A mile from here?"

Belle stared into the willows, visualizing a map of the Sagehen. "More like a mile and a half," she thought. She dog-trotted back to the north edge of the band. Beth came up to her and said, in a low, guilty voice, "Mounted men, sorry, I can't take that."

But for Belle, "mounted men" had a more complicated resonance. She knew that men stepped into saddles for a number of reasons, and the men came in diverse shapes and sizes. She thought about her own riders: Red, Brent, Henry. She remembered some of what she had told Henry, less than two hours ago. She remembered that Henry and Brent had ridden the Spring Gulch rapids in inner tubes. She said, "All right, let's throw them in the river."

They couldn't have come near to doing it without the dog and a favorable lay of the land: bottleneck in the south, shelving riverbanks, deep eddies. For Jack, it was routine: crowd the rear while herders work the van.

The women turned into merciless demons—pushing, shouting, lifting, leaping—in a panic. And the panic spread. The entire band began a vast side slippage that tumbled sheep into the river and the eddies fed sheep to fast water. The band became one mighty, complaining flow. There were a few times, near the end, when the weary herders came close to joining what they'd started.

The riders came, leather and horsehide scraping willows, hooves thudding on turfy ground. They spread out in the form of a rough crescent that was open to the river. They adjusted to the fact: no sheep, only three wet and muddy women who stood together, brushing at their clothing. No one spoke. Finally, Ruth and Belle and Beth looked up, one by one. Belle smiled; Ruth stared, defiantly; Beth frowned—and that's the way they appeared, two days later, on the front page of the *Sagehen Valley Courier.*

After making the exposure, Sylvester Matlock, Editor, climbed from his perch on a complacent pony that had been supplied by the OX. He turned to face the long frontage of horses, needing distance, in order to capture all in one frame. He had to back to the very edge of river water to get it.

JT said, "Well, ladies, you've been pretty bold. I'm not exactly sure about your motives in this, but you've certainly jumped right in and taken the bull by the horns."

Pancho Jones called out, "Sheep by the tail, JT," and growled an aside, "Asshole."

Abe Fox eased himself off his mare. JT stayed mounted. So did Horace Giles who still burned with memory of Jaimie on the ground, grabbing at his thigh, his hands soon bloodied. Giles had stood still, in disbelief; then, grief stricken, he had helped bandage Jaimie and went with him to the hospital. Now, he craved action, the rougher, the better. He waited impatiently for JT or Abe Fox—anybody—to get things moving. The butt of his saddle gun made short, sharp arcs as his horse, prodded by a restless rider, shifted about. Beth became fascinated by those motions. She felt a deep resentment.

Abe's attention faltered, he was adrift in other autumns. A serious problem, these driftings, but he hadn't found a way to prevent them. Now, leaning against his horse, soaking in the deep, rich heat of late morning, he was remembering Gabriel "Gramps" Fox. It had seemed a long journey, being with Gramps—several years of Abe's youth time—but Gramps' stories stretched those years, making contact with another century. Abe's interest had been strong. He took the trouble to divide Gramps' repertoire into "real truth" and "other stuff." It was mainly a matter of noting the intent of whatever tale Gramps had in hand, and the tone of his delivery. In nameless box canyons and open draws, in forgotten cow camps and dusty sheep folds, in desert places and paradise mountain meadows, there had been goings-on that were well worth the telling—many of them hilarious, some not so funny, some had gaps in them to cover things better left unsaid.

Abe came back, noted that Matlock had finished fooling around with his camera and that JT continued to look a trifle confused. "Can't decide if we've won or lost," Abe decided. It occurred to him that today would fade quickly and there would be a hundred different stories, and not one would be all "real truth." Some would be downright false.

He drifted again. A cold, windy morning in winter, Gramps up ahead on horseback, Abe following on a horse without a name other than "the old roan." Gramps leaned down from the saddle to open a gate, maneuvering his horse snug to the post, not wanting to step down into drifted snow. The horse objected, tossed its head, knocked its skull against Gramps' forehead. Gramps' hat went flying into the wind. He stood tall in the stirrups, gave one big yelp, his voice cracking. He swung down and chased the hat. When he remounted, he snugged his hat down and roared. The roar turned into squeaky laughter. He drew breath to get another run at the laugh. When he'd settled, he said, "By God, I'm ready now. This'll be a good day. You wait, you'll see."

Abe saw faces of friends. He gasped and reached into his pocket, but Amos Snow already had his own handkerchief ready, offering it. He put a hand on Abe's shoulder.

Lars Hamil asked, "You all right?"

Abe nodded, laughter lines still showing.

Lars said, "I thought you was having some kind of fit."

"I was... happened to think of something." Abe was aware of curious faces and the stamping of horses and flicking of horse tails against autumn flies. "Everything's fine," he said. "This will be a good day." He peered across the river and began to corner a few ideas. "Giles," he said, "how about you riding down river? Better cross over, the west side's easier. Take out all the sheep with cracked heads and busted legs. You got ammo?"

Giles nodded, pleased.

Abe glanced around. "How's that sound?"

Someone said, "So far, so good. I'm in favor. Don't want to let the woolies suffer."

A general discussion ensued. Abe waited. When Sandra looked at him and nodded, it made him happy. A good day.

Vienna Hamil said, "Somebody ought to go with Giles."

Shawn seconded that, told Giles to pick a partner. Giles gave the nod to Pancho Jones. They rode out, upstream, looking for a crossing.

Farny Burnham, a shirttail rancher from Two Creek, put the question that was in everybody's mind. "Are those sheep making it through the rapids? I'd guess that they are. My guess is they'll be coming ashore about where the river makes that big bend to the west."

"Some won't make it," Sandra said.

Abe said, "I believe we can wrap this up if we truck a few horses down to where the sheep come ashore. Suppose we were to round up the whole bunch and move them about six miles north by northwest."

Silence, everybody working out angles and distances. Sturling Crawford was the first to tumble. "That'd be this side of the Lizard, the Barrows grazing."

"I believe so," Abe said.

Lars Hamil looked south to where the Lizard seemed to swim in the heat. He began to see the picture: Abe had sent Giles to collect a transit tax. That was like Abe, do the important thing first, before a situation got discussed to death. The transit tax had been their main intent, all along. Well, if they decided to leave the damn sheep on federal land in the Sagehen, instead of pushing them back north, that had the virtue of saving them three or four days of pushing sheep. Besides, in a war you don't win everything. They'd raised a ruckus, now let JT do his bit, take care of the political end of things. Lars said, "I'll vote for that."

And now JT had worked it out. Silently, he gave Abe Fox full credit for taking hold of an unfortunate turn of events and fixing it up so that the cattlemen came out looking not too bad. They had gotten half a loaf, at least. The negative side was that Donnadio's damned animals would be preempting a prime piece of real estate. Smoke Creek and Far Haven would not be happy. More struggle lay ahead. Well, that was the name of the game.

Sylvester Matlock, in spite of—or because of—his years as a small town mugwump, had a well-honed knack of juggling trends and backlashes. A simile came to him and he couldn't keep it to himself. "Every sheep that ventures into this valley has to go through a Sagehen Dip," he said. "That's the way we play."

Someone asked, "Does that go on the front page, Sylvester?"

"I believe it might."

Belle Izard leaned close to Ruth and asked, "Are we co-opted, or not?"

"I believe we've won this hand. The sheep will be where we wanted them."

"Minus casualties. And more hands will be dealt, later."

"Enjoy this one."

Chapter 30

....

 JACK FORCED LAGGARDS into tight places where they found footing no cow would have attempted. The west bank was out of Jack's control, but he was way ahead of Horace Giles and Pancho Jones by at least two river curves and he was leaving the east side nearly clear of sheep. He ignored the few who lay in the rocks, on their sides, unable to rise. Among those that he brought to a joining with the main part of the band were several who humped along on three legs.

Jack flopped down and rested. He stayed alert. A herder would show up, sooner or later.

While Jack kept watch, Edward Gill, Sagehen's one lawyer, met with a judge in the Goshen courthouse on behalf of six men jailed overnight, charged with disorderly conduct and refusal to obey a law officer. Gill was a bumbler, but the judge made everything easy for him by keeping his interrogations brief and to the point. Gill paid the fines, from a fund that had been pledged, rather absentmindedly, by the cattlemen, whose attentions were focused elsewhere.

A seventh defendant, Evan Hughes, represented himself, paid from his own account. He fumed inside, not because of a sense of legal mismanagement—he could appreciate Sheriff Labray's inability to distinguish perpetrators from defenders—but from the absence of even token BLM backup.

Gill escorted his clients from the cool and dusky courthouse into hot Goshen glare. Evan hung back. He leaned against an Ionic column and sulked, but not for long. A dark, green sedan stopped at the courthouse steps and a stocky man stepped out, shaded his eyes and looked into the courthouse's entrance. He was dressed in full uniform, U. S. Forest Service. David Darwin, specialist in environmental evaluation and management.

Evan trotted down the steps. "Where the hell are my people?"

Dave gave him a "cool it" gesture. "Come on, Evan, let's go. BLM is full of concern for you —just a mite slow, that's all. Your District Manager, himself, was on his way here, but I volunteered. We need to talk."

They got into the car. Dave drove out of town and north on 11. "Your headquarters and mine have been in contact all along, from shortly after you disappeared. It wasn't until much later that any of us realized you had so rashly plunged into the DuckWing affair, all by your lonesome."

"Duty."

"Yes. Hey, I'm not criticizing." Dave chuckled while he chose his words. "I'm trying to indicate the general attitude. I know perfectly well why you took off on your own. We don't have to discuss it."

"Thanks, Dave. Could you bring me up to date?"

"Donnadio's foreman, Emanuel Gabriel, gave himself up. No gunplay. It wasn't John Moss who did the shooting, after all. How was your night in jail?"

"Conversations. Interesting. Yesterday I didn't do very well, Dave.

Should have taken Lashley out of that DuckWing scene, first thing. Instead, I hung around making futile gestures."

"Lashley?"

"He's the herder. Because of him being there, Jaimie went out of control, got himself shot. Later, in that stupid, mob fist fight, Lashley came up with some damage to three or four ribs. I called the hospital early this morning."

"Did you hear about those Sagehen women rescuing the sheep?"

"What are you talking about?"

"Three women, shoved the whole band into the river. The sheep ran the rapids." Dave smiled, thinking about it.

Evan looked at him. "You're kidding."

"No, it happened. The women... I've got their names."

"Was one of them Ruth Zalent?"

"That seems to ring a bell."

"I begin to believe you. Where are the sheep?"

"They landed somewhere north of Blackrock. That's all I have on it. I've been tied up with paperwork. Another directive came down the line. Nothing new, just an underlining of the last one."

"Strongly suggest recommend land exchange, soonest."

"You got it, nearly word for word. Packard had the courtesy to give it to me over the phone." He slowed the car to 55 mph. It was a big moment for him. "I dis-recommended it."

"You didn't!"

"Sure as hell did."

Evan was struck dumb, he opened his mouth, shut it.

Dave said, "I know you've always figured me as a sort of go-along-to-get-along." He smiled.

Evan thought about it. "At times. No, that's not quite right. More the gutsy go-by-the-book type."

"Well, same thing."

"No, not the same thing."

"Anyway, here's what happened. I re-surveyed all the data we have on the north boundary region of the Jedediah, came across a document that couldn't be overlooked. Some range con, maybe your predecessor, had done a meticulous forage survey up there. He gave it a rating of 'Poor,' of course, but added a footnote, bless the man. 'Nibbled to the ground,' he wrote, 'crustose lichens trampled into dust, cheat grass taking over, worst range I've ever seen.'"

"I've been in the general area, told you about it."

"No offense, Evan, but this was down-on-the-ground counting and analysis. It's always nice to have data. I concluded that, on the basis of evidence at hand and upon due consideration of current grazing lease commitments and levels of stocking, and so on, blah, blah—the proposed land swap has to be judged unacceptably unbalanced."

"You'll be overruled. You know that."

"Of course I know that. No doubt I'll be slated for transfer, too."

"Maybe, maybe not. Why did you do this?"

"The facts were lying there on the desk, staring me in the face. I'm a paper hound, Evan; you know that; anything in print makes me sit up and take notice. I sat there staring at it, that's all. Wasn't any choice, really. Evelyn's taking it really well. Actually, it's the kids I worry about. They're both of them finally adjusted to Goshen. They actually like it, at the moment. Can you beat that?"

"We'll fight this, Dave."

"I know. That's the hell of it. Can't back down, but don't look so eager. And let's not get all broody and hostile about it, OK? That was Evelyn's advice. I recommend it. One day at a time. Look, you've had a tough twenty-four hours. Take the day off, read a book."

"I'll take a shower."

"All right, then come over for supper tonight."

"You better check with Evelyn."

"She suggested it. By the way, a woman called from Aspen. She's at one of those high-tone save-the-world conferences. You're to call her."

"Who is she?"

"A lawyer, that's all I know. Lila something. I wrote it down."

"I don't know any Lilas."

"Apparently this Sagehen situation made network TV, late last night. I didn't catch it, this woman did. Remind me to give you her phone number."

"Why me?"

"Because she wants to talk to somebody knowledgeable about the Sagehen. That's you. 'Soon as he gets out of jail,' I told her."

Chapter 31

··

 LINC SUTTON DROVE into the hospital's half-circle drive, late in the day. Bryan Lashley hustled from the reception room and climbed into the pickup, awkwardly. He had tape across the bridge of his nose, and he'd lost his hat. Linc asked if he was in pain.

"Some. My ribs are taped. As long as I breathe slow and easy, I'm all right."

"Busted ribs?"

"They say it's cartilage damage."

Linc drove with caution, a black pipe clamped in a corner of his mouth. "Manny rode into the ranch, a little before noon," he said. "He's the one shot the cowboy."

"I was thinking it was John Moss. Damn! This is bad."

"Gino called the sheriff's office and arranged for Manny to give himself up. Gino's on the rampage—fired his lawyer, gone on the prowl for another one."

"We need a good lawyer, the best."

Linc was silent, intent on the sparse Goshen traffic.

Lashley said, "That cowboy, Jaimie, he went crazy. He was set to shoot me down, point blank. I was looking death right in the eye. Manny knew it. Jaimie's the one at fault. Put that in your pipe and keep it there."

Once on the highway, Linc increased speed and held the old truck steady at thirty-five. Bryan thought, "Christ, we'll be half the night," but he didn't complain. He gave Linc a full account of the sheep drive and its ending in disaster at the DuckWing. Linc smiled; he was sitting on news of his own. At Blackrock, he turned into the parking space in front of Ma Grenville's.

"I can't afford this, Linc," Lashley said. "Besides, I need a bath."

They sat in the cab for a few moments. Linc put his pipe away. "I missed lunch. I'll pay."

They went in. A smiling waitress led them to a corner table and offered menus. They declined and ordered coffee, hot roast beef, and apple pie. Bryan watched her walk away. A terrible pang of desire came over him. His ribs hurt and his head ached and his nose felt like it was made out of fiberboard. He was on the edge of feeling sorry for himself when Linc said, "You'll be in the lap of luxury down here, Bryan." He swept a hand across the tablecloth and the silverware and onward to include the room—the bustle, the aromas of food cooked out of sight and brought forth by women, a place of women's voices, their footsteps, their presence.

"What are you talking about?" Bryan asked.

Linc showed most of his stained teeth. "Seems your sheep got thrown in the Sagehen River and rode down to a pretty fair landing, someplace north of here. The cowmen drove them over to the Barrows lease and went on home. That BLM man called up Gino, let him know."

Lashley leaned across the tablecloth, pushed a finger toward Linc. "That kind of stuff happens in storybooks."

Linc pulled a long, owlish look. "Would BLM lie?"

"Come on, Linc, don't play around."

"I've told you the truth." He looked pleased—such a rare sight, Lashley believed him. "What's Gino say?"

"Says Clarence can bring the wagon and supplies, stay with you a few days, help you get set up—unless you're too banged up."

"I'm OK."

"If you're too banged up, I'm to bring you in."

"We got to find Jack."

Linc shrugged. "I imagine he's with his sheep. We'll see. Nothing's nailed down for sure, down here. You got to understand that. For all you know, the feds'll kick you out next week. If not them, the cowmen."

They had seconds on coffee and sat in solid enjoyment, waiting for pie. "If they take a notion to," Linc said, "cow people can go to work and get used to sheep in their territory. They've done it before, other places."

"You know, that John Moss, he's been a cowman all his life, and I count him as pretty much a friend. What's the word on him?"

"There was some talk, where I got gas in Sagehen. Something about Moss riding off into the Heeaws, something about a wonder horse. That's all I can tell you."

Lashley smiled. "You know, Linc, I kind of enjoy the idea of John pesticating around out there."

"A man gets to roaming, gets trouble."

The waitress was bringing their pie. She was slight and dark and had her hair in a ponytail. "Trouble," Lashley said, "I suppose that's part of it." Linc made a faint growling noise, more a sign of contentment than anything else. Bryan persisted. "I do enjoy the idea," he said. He studied the dining room, gathering the scene for thinking about later. Soon, Linc would light his pipe and it would be time to go look for Jack.

Chapter 32

....

 AT ABOUT MIDNIGHT, Brownie walked into a narrow, mountain meadow. Detecting no particular urging from his rider, he stopped and put his muzzle into lush frostbitten herbage. He stepped occasionally, syncopated pivotings, casual and massive. There were stars above, no sounds from the woods and the backtrail utterly silent. Winds from timberline came into the meadow as playful hums and whisperings.

John, bone tired, stayed in the saddle, doing nothing. Memories came easily. Other midnights, other meadows. They gave way to an insistent flickering glare—fluorescent lights, a howling wind—Goshen Airport, February blizzard slackening, still drumming and tugging on the metal building. Sarah and John were in the waiting room, their final scene, John smoking.

He muttered, deliberately and with malice, that a man waited for her. A man in Denver. No need to lie about it.

She slapped him. His cigarette skittered across the floor. He chased it. When he returned to his seat, he sat up straight—the better to look down his nose at the stares of the other passengers. There were five of those, all strangers.

"I'm sorry," Sarah said, "but don't you call me a liar. You are my man."

How could she lay claim to him, and be leaving? He asked—it was an old, moth-eaten question—if the problem wasn't simply that they had no children, and never would.

"No, not to my knowledge," she said. "You can get all psychological about it, if you want to. I'm sick and tired of it, everybody hovering around about that."

They sat in silent, mutual misery. "Remember that doctor?" she said, in a milder tone.

"Huh! Not likely I'd forget." The second doctor had been helpful and matter-of-fact, confirming what the first doctor had told them. The funny thing was that he spoke in alternations—to her, to him, to her—never to both. Later, they'd laughed. John fumed over the doctor saying "uterus" when speaking to Sarah and "womb" when speaking to him.

It had taken about two years to find out and admit that they would not be having babies. They adjusted and went on with their life, running the Barrows ranch. Those were the partnership years, working outside—clearing ditches, fixing fences, irrigating, baling hay, managing animals. They were efficient workers, and Hal Barrows wasn't stingy when it came to buying equipment and shelling out for maintenance. Sarah and John began to have time on their hands. Sarah took long rides, exploring the east slopes of the Jedediahs and the desert to the south, and she talked to Evan Hughes about her discoveries. Her conversations with him renewed a crusading enthusiasm that had lain dormant since the night she had rejected her environmental lawyer. She knew Evan Hughes' reputation—"as red as he is green." But that didn't mean she couldn't happen to run into him once in a while and have a relaxed trading of views on the state of the world and its wild critters.

She became an activist. Belle Izard and a few others joined her in writing letters on behalf of threatened species, but it wasn't long before they realized they were working to save habitats, and that meant land and that meant conflict too close to home.

John defended Sarah, good-naturedly and without strain. He enjoyed talking up coyotes in front of certified coyote haters, such as Shawn Lynch. But for Sarah, everything was going downhill. She led the fight against the Instar Gold Mine, and lost. She began to see, everywhere, victories turning partial, defeats becoming outright, final and devastating. Her friends were concerned. Sarah was becoming too rigid, too intense. They made allowances. Childless, she had special needs. They wrapped their impatience in kindness, wanting her to be happy.

John kept on agreeing with her. That came easily to him. He was one of those cowmen who want the whole shebang—cattle, grizzly bears, Lahontan trout—and saw no reason why all couldn't be accommodated. That was not Sarah's view. They argued about it, and he began to urge her to ease up. "It's not all bad, Sarah. Besides, you're not responsible for the whole world. Dammit, woman, I want you to be happy."

But she was hearing another voice from him—silent, unexamined: "Your work is less serious than other kinds. It doesn't have strict deadlines, like getting the cattle on the trucks. It is, in short, second-rate." That voice was always there, obscuring and downgrading everything else that he said or did. It was driving her from him. It was one more thing that could not be laid out in the open. "I'll be damned if I'll beg," became her attitude. She created for herself a certain aloof dignity, the only refuge left to her. She became taciturn, joined him in his lifelong aversion to wordy heart-to-heart discussion.

Then came rumors of Far Haven, and Sarah shrank from the challenge. She had few allies, after that struggle with Instar, and her sturdy defender, her man, couldn't—wouldn't?—see her desperation. Winter came; she knew that spring was too far away. She would run to Denver, find a dumb job, and wait for hope.

But in the waiting room at Goshen Airport, at the end, she did speak. She began with a mountain—she and two friends climbing through rim-rock and dangling their feet over a buffalo drop, a place where people, long before horse culture, drove buffalo over the cliff. "I was in a romantic mood, just out of high school, coming up for air. Imagine us three young women on those cliffs, taking off our shirts, standing bare-bosomed, holding our arms out. It's lucky one of us didn't get blown over the edge. We sunned ourselves on big rock slabs. You see it? We three, in that huge, old, old place? So powerful! Wind, sun, rock, we were with the power."

"Even dumb cowpokes take their shirts off, once in a while," he said. He smiled, staring at the floor.

"I know that, and there might come a time when you wear out that 'dumb cowpoke' cover."

"What a fucked-up situation," he thought. "Why didn't we talk like this before now?"

"At the buffalo drop," she continued, "I made up scenes of those people working the buffalo. I had them signaling to each other. I made up expressions on their faces. Some of them jumped up, yelling and waving skin shirts. They were real to me; I was with them, a feather in my hair. Later, I tried to imagine thousands of years of their ways of doing things—couldn't, it's not possible. The crash is all we know. In a few years, it was all over for them. I saw modern times going crash, too. It might happen quicker than we ever suppose, like with those others who lived here—where Goshen Airport is now."

"I've thought that, too," he said.

"You have?" But she was still wrapped in her own story. "Last year, all the talk about Far Haven and people fussing over the ranching way of life and how it was threatened—I remembered that day with the buffalo people. I saw that when a way of life gets to where it has to be preserved, one part of me says it's maybe time to let it die."

"You try to preserve species, why not ways of life?"

"You've hit on a very tough point—or should I say tender?"

"Huh?"

"Why fight for grizzlies or wolves or peregrine falcons or family ranches? Have you ever really asked yourself? I have. I didn't find an answer. Not in words. Maybe not at all."

"You didn't?"

"I'm leveling with you. I do want the grizzlies to hang in with us, for whatever time is left, but so what? What sense does it make?"

"Jesus, I thought you knew!"

She laughed, softly, scarcely twelve inches from him. "I no longer know much of anything, for sure."

He had a glimmer of hope, and now, in the saddle, listening to Brownie tear and chew, he looked again at that glimmer, the thought that maybe Sarah wasn't sure about leaving the Sagehen, leaving her man. And he remembered her next words: "That big conference on Greater Yellowstone Ecosystem. No answers. A real downer."

"Yes," he said, "you had a bad time there."

"Very bad. So many people at the conference acted like there was time to study and carry out some perfectly tippy-toe strategy and all the time, everybody knew there wasn't enough time. When the last bear is dead, there are no more. Simple as that. So, if you're short of time, what is to be done? Isn't that a logical question?"

He evaded it. "I remember you were pretty well pissed off."

"I didn't tell you everything. On the way home, I stopped for gas and coffee and decided there was no sense paying for a motel. I was too wrought up. I kept on driving. You know that rough country, this side of Beulah? I saw a buffalo."

"That's mainly sheep country, down around Beulah," he said. "Some deer, no buffalo."

"A mile or two from where the road comes out of the canyon is where I saw him. Very tall at the shoulders. Right up against a bunch of deerbrush. A bull. He stood side-on to me."

John shook a cigarette out of the pack, then put it back. "You'd have to go quite a ways from Beulah to find buffalo. Jackson Hole, Denver Zoo."

"His eye gleamed, his head turned. He looked at me."

"How fast were you going?"

"Around forty-five, I suppose. It's a slow road. By the time I found a safe place to turn around, I decided not to. I'd seen him and was sure of it, and it was way past midnight."

"Was there talk about buffalo, up at the conference?"

"Some, nothing particular. I was getting pretty sleepy, I admit that. You think it was deerbrush lighted up a certain way, in the headlights."

His reply caught him by surprise. "Maybe not deerbrush, Sarah. Maybe a vision."

She shifted and glanced at him, for the first time. "Are you humoring me? I never told this to you—not to anybody. I thought...."

"You saw a buffalo," he said. "A true vision, Sarah. That's what I think."

Her response was drowned by a sudden roaring from outside—the flight to Denver. Lights flashed against the windows and the outer doors flung open. Two men in coveralls came in, and the loudspeaker told passengers what to do. Sarah stood, whispered a word and joined the line that was already moving quickly into the storm. She looked back, once.

John entertained a brief resentment at the way Brownie kept nosing across the meadow as if the world was one big picnic and he had perfect access to all of it.

"We'll make a cold camp," he said, and swung down and led Brownie to a dry, level place at the east end of the meadow.

Later, lying on his back under blankets, he pondered the grizzly-bear question and found an answer. In the morning, he couldn't recall it.

Jasper Pass, by noon. Winter wind and a gigantic view. Dry country, low hills and ridges, all under a horde of fast-moving clouds. John stood in the lee of the horse, chilled to the bone. A U.S. Air Force sign warned against unauthorized travel farther east. Three choices, then: Go north or south or traipse back to the Sagehen.

"What do I know about Sarah, my wife?" Brownie shifted, wanting to get his back against the wind. "The point is," John continued, "Sarah has adventures; she's been that way, all her life." It was a new thought, allowing others. He mounted and rode into the partial shelter of a whitebark pine. He looked out past the sign. "Funny," he said, "I always thought I was the one."

In the south, a raven rose on an updraft. In that direction, far and away, was Highway 6 out of Beulah, and beyond Beulah, a way to Denver.

"What do you think, horse?" With very slight pressure on the left neck rein, he gave Brownie a hint.